The
Annunciationist

Kenneth Kuenster

The Annunciationist

A Novel

Addison & Highsmith

Addison & Highsmith Publishers

Las Vegas ◊ Chicago ◊ Palm Beach

Published in the United States of America by
Histria Books
7181 N. Hualapai Way, Ste. 130-86
Las Vegas, NV 89166 USA
HistriaBooks.com

Addison & Highsmith is an imprint of Histria Books. Titles published under the imprints of Histria Books are distributed worldwide.

Library of Congress Control Number: 2021937710

ISBN 978-1-59211-105-3 (hardcover)
ISBN 978-1-59211-197-8 (softbound)
ISBN 978-1-59211-272-2 (eBook)

To

Pia

Part One

The Paintings

Twenty-one hours after leaving Brindisi, meandering from port to port, our ship docks in the shadow of the high crest of the island, bringing me and my obsession to Santorini. This is my first trip to this dramatic island, which lies at the southern edge of the Cyclades Archipelago. Only Crete lies between it and the coast of North Africa.

I'm here at the invitation of Orlando Pettingill, who owns a villa on the island. He and I are old friends. I'm a painter and he's a collector of art. He divides his time between a mansion on the north coast of California, where I'd only known him before, and here. This division of time and location reflects contrasting sides of this gifted and fascinating man, as I'm to learn on this odyssey.

My obsession: Why, in an Annunciation painting when I see the Archangel Gabriel kneeling before the Virgin, delivering the word of God on the subject of who's in her womb, do I, arch agnostic, feel such empathy, even responsibility, not only for Gabriel and the Virgin but for the whole intimate exchange? And more to the point, why when I observe Annunciations, do I feel so poignantly the pain of my history of lost love. When I mentioned this in a letter to Orlando, he responded, "Well my friend, after you've traveled the length of Italy observing Annunciations, come here to work it out."

To reach Orlando's villa I take a fishing boat from the port, and I'm delivered by a taciturn fisherman to a pier on Orlando's private peninsula.

I step onto a stone wharf and watch the fishing caique rumble away trailed by its widening V tinted crimson by the bright twilit sky. Silhouetted against the sky is the volcanic island that sits opposite Santorini. From the dark shape of this Vulcan that still releases wisps of steam and smoke, I look up behind me to the sheer crescent of Santorini rising hundreds of feet above. Following instructions, I pull on a blue rope alongside cables anchored in the stone wharf. I hear a distant gonging and stand in a shaded alcove of the stone wall. In a few minutes an ornate elevator cage descends and stops a few inches above my eye level. Squatting inside and peering out through the decorative metalwork is a pale blond boy wearing only a white T-shirt. I step out from the shade.

"Who are you? I was expecting Cook."

He says this in very British English. I explain that I've been invited by Orlando to visit the villa. Then we both hear the approach of another caique. A young, very dark Greek girl steps onto the wharf. The fisherman hands over baskets of fruit, vegetables, bread, milk, cheese, and departs. The girl looks at me with a puzzled frown, then shouts impatiently in Greek at the elevator that the boy has raised a few feet. He descends to the wharf, steps out and loads in the baskets.

As we go up in the elevator, the girl removes a white neck scarf and abruptly ties it around the boy's upright penis, and says something chastise-sounding in Greek. Then she smiles at me and continues to watch me with the darkest irises I've ever seen. Her hair is straight and black, her features are strong, and she has a faint black mustache above her wide amused mouth. She has three moles on her left cheek, like islands across an olive sea. As I watch her watch me, out of the corner of my eye I see the white scarf twitch twice in small waves of surrender.

The elevator stops at a concrete platform surrounded by a blue railing. We are several hundred feet above the sea and the uninterrupted view out over the Aegean and its islands is spectacular. The path to the steps of the villa is intricately inlaid in circular patterns of round stones and to the sides are mazes of poppies and lavender and rosemary.

The boy leads the way up the path in a jaunty step, still wrapped in Cook's kerchief, until he sees a tall man in a gray suit emerge from the shadows of the villa entry. He puts down his baskets and darts back behind us to reappear quickly, wearing khaki shorts that he must have ditched on his way down to meet Cook at the wharf. Cook and the boy pass the man and the boy says with careful deference, "Hello Father."

"Hello Reginald, airing things out a bit, were we?" Then he turns to me.

"Sir?"

I introduce myself and explain that I've been invited by Orlando to visit.

"Ah yes, we're expecting you," He bows slightly and says, "Mr. Pettingill is in Hong Kong. I am Hamm, welcome to Santorini."

I am led by Hamm through a maze of cool dim hallways, through light open spaces and hallways again. The villa is built onto and into the cliff and seems endless. There is art everywhere. Bathed in light is a row of Classic Greek torsos. "Originals, not Roman copies," explains Hamm.

Across a creamy marble floor are a red Bokhara, and a Picasso rug. Two Picasso paintings on a wall as well, and an early Sienese Madonna, a Brâncuși sculpture, and a thick sensuous bronze Maillol. As I follow Hamm through this collection of museum class art, I wonder how it all came into Orlando's possession. I've only seen his collection in California, which is mostly focused on North American modern art. I knew of his broad interest in all art, but the connoisseurship behind this collection is stunning.

I ask Hamm, "Does Orlando have advisors in his buying of art and in the display of it here?"

Hamm stops to answer, "Mr. Pettingill has personally chosen every object in his collection and he has decided on the precise placement of every piece here. Right now, he is in Hong Kong to acquire the fourth and final bowl of an ancient quartet of Chinese bowls he has pursued over a decade. The other three bowls are displayed downstairs."

Hamm then proceeds to relate to me the provenance of many of the objects we pass as we continue on our tour. His knowledge of art is far beyond the qualifications of head butler, as he'd be called in his native England, or as overseer of the villa as he refers to himself here on Santorini.

"Hamm, you seem to have a strong background in art and museum matters."

I am curious about this obviously intelligent and knowledgeable man, and also his odd, horny little adolescent son Reginald, and how they came to be here.

Hamm stops before speaking.

"I was educated in the history of art. I was the curator of the collection of some Arab royalty before Mr. Pettingill acquired me along with a few pieces from the Prince's collection some years ago."

Hamm stops before a door, pushes it open and says, "I hope you will find this room to your liking."

He bows slightly and walks back down the hall.

My room has a simple graceful brass bed, a primitive painted Spanish armoire, a thick sacristy table, and on the walls, a Russian ikon and a Modigliani nude drawing. There is a large terrace with a cluster of freestanding ancient marble columns of various heights like a fluted petrified forest. Looking out past the columns at the expanse of various blues, I feel a sudden rush of desire to create, to draw and to paint. I hear a slight clink and turn to see Cook placing a tea tray on the table. She stares for a moment with an enigmatic smile, then turns and goes out the door.

The villa has no routine I'm told by Hamm except dinner and then only when Orlando is in residence. Cook, it turns out is just that, not chef. She assists Francesco, the artist of the kitchen. He is pleased to see me because the villa is almost empty, its social season beginning with Orthodox Easter, several weeks away. The only other guests at present are a pair of East German twins, performance artists whom Orlando met and invited to the villa after seeing them perform in Berlin. To chef Francesco's frustration, the twins are thin ascetic vegetarians.

I settle into a routine. After fruit, yogurt, and coffee served by Cook with a grin that obliterates her three moles like a tidal wave, I spend the morning in my studio. On the ferry from Italy, I'd drawn innumerable Gabriels and Virgins as I thought about the strong effect on me of the Annunciations I'd seen. My feeling in Italy was that I could have, even should have painted them myself. It's the curious relationship between the Archangel Gabriel and the Virgin that fascinates me. On the surface it's a matter of a somewhat detached looking messenger delivering his/her message. But, consider the message: "Hello, I'm here at the behest of God, to tell you something about your womb. Now please excuse me for offering this delicate observation but I know something about you, you don't know." Now how could Gabriel not feel intimately connected to the Virgin after saying something like that? Didn't he in effect, in a roundabout way, make her pregnant? She wasn't aware of a pregnancy before he appeared. And didn't the presence of a white dove, and a white lily, make it all sort of sweetly abstract? Innocently abstract? And the fact that she was reading a book, an everyday thing, make it all a somewhat bland context for so momentous an event? Gabriel is unquestionably a major player in this, and I find myself strongly identifying with him, or more accurately wishing to identify with him. Whenever I've been drawn to become close to someone, I've always felt a great gap in my capacity to connect, as though it would take an almost mystical intervention to bring about a closeness that I've always coveted but never achieved. That is something that fascinates me about the Annunciation: the parallel between my longing, as artist and man, and this creative act on the part of the archangel, and if everything that followed wasn't a grand work of art, what is?

***

Days slip by uncounted as I draw, and think, and wander about the villa carefully examining the paintings and sculpture accumulated by this brilliant and obsessive collector who has established this museum in this remote villa. My mind is gradually emptied of the clutter of my previous lonely existence in the U.S. I'm entering a realm where my mind is open to what comes next in my world.

Suddenly filling the void, verbally and physically, is Orlando who has returned from the far East. He pokes his large head into my studio doorway. I have not seen him in two years, and, as always, I'm unprepared for the impact of his appearance. Orlando has a large head, great protruding watery eyes, massive jowls, and a complexion with a slight cast of pale green. I hesitate to use the word that always comes to mind to describe my friend, but no other will do. Orlando is like a giant frog.

"May I?", he says, after we embrace, gesturing toward my studio.

He walks into the center of the room and turns slowly, looking at my many Virgins and Gabriels. The only sound in the room is Orlando's breathing, as his great jowls inflate and deflate. He turns to grace me with the Cheshire smile he reserves for acknowledgment of an event in the realm of art.

"Martin, I see what you meant in your letter about the effect on you of the Italian Annunciations. Something is unfolding, but what is it?" He works his jowls while waiting for my answer.

"What's unfolding is a need to paint my own Annunciations."

He watches me with narrowed speculating eyes and says, "A brilliant anachronism." When he sees my slight frown, he immediately adds, "By that I mean anachronism in the eyes of the world in general. You and I both know that there are no anachronisms in art. Come downstairs and see what I've brought back from Hong Kong."

We look at four bowls in a glass case. "They couldn't be more modern, don't you agree?"

He is right. The shapes are simple and elegant and the very minimal decorations could have been done by Picasso or Matisse.

He goes on, "But here's the interesting part. The visual beauty belies the history behind the bowls. These four bowls were chosen by a Ming Dynasty emperor in the sixteenth century, out of dozens made by a young artist whom he had chosen, that perfectly represented the four seasons. The remaining bowls were ordered destroyed by the emperor so that only these, signifying his infallible eye, remained. The artist was locked in a room with the other bowls until he destroyed them, which he refused to do and subsequently starved to death. The bowls were loaded aboard a junk along with the body of the young artist and consigned to the China Sea."

We both silently look at the bowls and reflect on their story.

"So, my dear friend, I wonder what story your Annunciations will tell."

"And I wonder the same thing, Orlando."

I'm relieved to have Hamm appear, rolling in a cart of gin, ice, lemon peel, and more. He opens glass doors at the end of the gallery and wheels the cart out onto a terrace furnished with cushioned rattan chairs. Orlando and I sit back and the icy silver of gin followed by a Santorini olive, dollop of feta, and a few pistachios nicely push the Ming bowls and my Annunciations into the background. We silently take in the spectacle of the sun setting over the islands. Orlando gestures out over the water to the smaller islands of Nea Kameni and Theresia that were part of Santorini before the catastrophic volcanic eruption of the fifteenth century B.C.

"Atlantis", he says softly.

After a few moments of silence, he goes on, "A Greek archeologist set forth the theory that Santorini is the site of Plato's Atlantis. Under his direction, in 1966, a marine expedition, here in the waters surrounding Santorini, took seismic readings establishing that the volcanic event here corresponded exactly to the details of Plato's account of the disappearance of Atlantis, including the tidal waves that destroyed the coastal civilizations of Crete. When I'm here in the villa, Martin, I never doubt that the man was right. I can feel it and in time I believe you will too."

***

The next morning as I'm looking through my drawings, I'm still thinking about the Ming bowls and their tale of death, and Plato's Atlantis and the possibility that I'm sitting above an ancient city wiped out by floods. All that darkness, and I begin to think of my impending Annunciation and I realize two things: My Gabriel and my Virgin must be drawn from real life, with real people for models, and there must be an element of darkness, partly to reflect my own ambiguity about passionately connecting and what is consequently concealed in the shadows of my view of life. Then, thinking of Gabriel, I think darkness literally and the image of Cook comes to mind. Wouldn't she be an appropriate model for my archangel?

I explain to Hamm that I'd like him to ask Cook if she'd be interested in being a model for my drawing in her off time for a wage. Since Cook appears to speak almost no English, I need his aid.

"Certainly," Hamm says as though it's as ordinary a request as asking for milk with my tea.

That evening, I'm on my balcony sipping ouzo, my mind as distant as the horizon I'm contemplating. I hear a soft sound behind me and I turn to see Cook standing primly, her feet together, her hands clasped behind her back, her head tipped down and her eyes under partly closed lids watching me carefully. She is naked. I'm puzzled by her nudity and wonder if I miscommunicated with Hamm. I'm about to try and convey to Cook that I wished to draw her clothed. But I don't because there is a quality of Ming Dynasty death and Atlantis disaster in her dark hairy self that I would never have expected. I'm mesmerized as I convert her in my mind to the role of archangel Gabriel. I study her wordlessly.

Her body is gracefully round and her waist and ankles are small. Her breasts are full and her dark nipples have a halo of fine black hair. Her belly protrudes slightly and there is a fine line of hair from her navel to her triangle, and a trail of soft black hair descends the insides of her thighs. The slight mustache above her mouth now seems both normal and intimate. If I hadn't been dazed by the ouzo and my emerging vision of Gabriel, I would have reacted more quickly. I simply sit and look. Cook turns and presents herself from the side. Her head is still down and her eyes are on mine. Then she turns her back to me and, planting her feet apart, puts her hands on her firm hips and looks up and to the side as though getting bored.

"Cook..." I softly say.

She turns to face me. She looks up, her dark eyebrows together, as though searching for her words on the ceiling.

"OK, you picture me?"

"Yes, Cook, you'll be superb to draw, to picture." I nod to be sure she understands.

She grins and quickly turns back into my room. She emerges dressed as usual in black peasant blouse and skirt. Her feet are bare and slap happily as she comes out on the balcony to sit before me, pleased.

"I don't know your name."

"Cook."

"No, your given name."

She guesses correctly at what I'm asking, and says something in Greek. I say, "In English?"

"An-gel-ika."

I stare again, stunned, motionless, then apologize.

"I'm sorry, it's just too much a coincidence, you see I want to draw you and paint you as an angel, the Archangel Gabriel, a dark archangel."

Angelika smiles and raises her hands, palms up, fingers spread, which is to be her 'I don't understand a word you've said' gesture.

"When picture me?"

"Draw you."

"Draw you?"

"Never mind, tomorrow."

I look to see if she understands, and she nods. I point to my watch, "Same time?"

She nods, and leaves.

It all happened so fast and now I sit in my ouzo daze with a rapidly rising euphoria at being able to start drawing so soon and with such a curiously intriguing model. But why had she presented herself nude? It would never have occurred to me to ask that of her. In fact, my image of the dark archangel was Angelika in her usual black clothing, and with black wings. But now that I've seen her in all her dark hairy nakedness, I know that Angelika nude with some sort of black wings is exactly the presence I want in my Annunciation. It's as though she guessed at my concealed image.

The next morning, with the translating aid of Reginald, I convey to Angelika that I want her to buy some black fabric in town for wings. I ask for this help from Reginald to ease the resentment he's shown toward me since my arrival. I sense he sees me as a rival for Angelika's attention and I want to make friends with him. He stands close to Angelika, happily doing the translation, while his nostrils celebrate her various scents.

That evening, Angelika is on the floor of the studio and I am above her on a stepladder, drawing. She is on her left side, right leg out front, knee bent, left leg in a curve behind her. Her right arm is forward, elbow bent, her fingers in the prescribed Annunciation gesture. The wings I've made from the black fabric flare out behind her. They consist of strips cut with rounded ends that converge as they approach her body. Angelika's expression and gesture are perfect for her assertive delivery of the dark archangel's message. I had showed her my drawings of Gabriel from my Italian travels and she immediately began to mime the poses and gestures of those angels. I realize that she is not only highly motivated to be a perfect Gabriel but also is very perceptive and sensitive to imagery. I can't believe my luck.

This is the second drawing of the evening. I will also draw her on her back.

On her back, Angelika has relaxed her legs, one knee slightly bent, releasing a subtle scent of sex, and with her hands out front, a sweaty sweetness is freed from the dark under her arms. A rosemary rinse she uses on her hair wafts through the animal odors. This mix of sex, sweat, and herb forms an aura that envelopes me as I draw, and the mood in the room is that this is no intellectual endeavor. I'm pleased that Angelika is bringing so much to her role on her own. As I observe her, I feel looked upon, looked into. I feel like she knows something I don't know. Or, perhaps she knows something I do know, that she is a stand-in for me. She is wearing her enigmatic smile. I wish I could speak Greek so I could talk to her.

I say, "Let's rest a while."

I sit back on top of the ladder. Angelika gets up from the floor and climbs two steps up the ladder. Her face is playful but challenging. I know she wishes she could say something. Then she does in Greek. First a few tentative sentences, all the while looking directly into my eyes. Then she unleashes a Greek chorus lament that goes on and on. It's obvious I have no idea what she's saying, but that doesn't seem to bother her. When she's finished she silently stares at me. Finally, I gesture for her to lie back down, which she does and I arrange her into another position. Her scents are richer than before. It's necessary for me to arrange her limbs to position her. She responds to this with total compliance, like her body's a pliable material for sculpture. I'm uncomfortable that I like touching her. When she's in the position I want, I smile and say, "Good", and I climb back up the ladder. I continue to draw for two more hours, making several more drawings that I feel are leading somewhere. Out of all this nonverbal (in that we don't understand each other's words) communication we've begun to agree on what we're doing here together, and her contribution is uncanny.

When I draw, I expend intense energy, and when I'm finally ready to stop, I'm exhausted. I spread out the drawings on the floor and we both look at them. Taking a cue from Angelika I begin to talk enthusiastically about various drawings, knowing she can't understand me and not caring. Suddenly I'm exhausted and lightheaded and I lie down on the floor over some black wing material. I'm sticky from the heat and from my drawing. Angelika kneels down watching me carefully and then lies next to me. We are on our backs and watch a small pink lizard on the ceiling shoot out its tongue twice, collecting its insect dinner. I slip into a deep sleep, with Angelika sleeping next to me, our bodies not touching. I'm awakened several hours later, by Angelika climbing over me as short cut to the bathroom. Sections of black wing are pressed against her naked back and bottom. I sit up and see bits of wing wrapped around my thigh. 'Some celestial event' is the thought that comes to mind. At the door, Angelika, back in her clothes, gives me a finger wiggling wave and leaves. I sleep the remaining hours till dawn imagining that I hear one declaration after another in Greek, offering more information about the true nature and purpose of this Annunciation, and my role in it.

Angelika and I work together most evenings for two or three hours. I'm excited by the drawings. I've used thick black conte on large sheets of paper and the dark intensity of Gabriel strikes out from the drawings. In two weeks, there are dozens of drawings taped to the walls of the studio. I no longer think of her as Angelika; now, she is Gabriel, and she knows it, and since she also seems part me, does that make me part Gabriel?

***

Early one morning, walking barefoot on the cool marble floor of a meandering hallway where I haven't been before, I pass a door open a few inches and catch a quick glimpse of bare flesh. I back up to look in. It's a large high-ceilinged room filled with indirect morning light. A large thick wood cross is at an angle on the floor. I see no one. Then a very thin naked body in a slow turning dance moves from the side toward the cross, immediately followed by another. The first, a male, rolls onto the vertical of the cross. The second, a female as thin as the first, rolls over him on her stomach. In a slow series of movements, accompanied by a low, dirge-like lament in German from both of them, he raises his hand to the horizontal of the cross and she does the same, placing hers over his. Then his right hand goes up to the horizontal and hers does the same. Their heads are tipped down, their long blond curly hair dangling over their shoulders. They form a perfect crucifix. After a few seconds of low moan, they roll to the side and fall to the floor, he on top, their limbs awry.

I retreat silently down the hall. So, these are the East German twins, the performance artists? They are thin to the point of emaciation. Their bodies so un-fleshy, I thought at first that they were both male, her hips so narrow and her breasts so small. His slack penis, and her absence of same, the only clue to gender. I have been at the villa two weeks and this is the first I've seen of them. They don't appear for meals and Hamm tells me they grow sprouts in jars and grasses in soil-filled boxes.

Two days later, there is a knock on my studio door. I open it to find the twins, unclothed.

In heavily accented, but perfect English, the brother says, "We have heard about your drawings and ask if we might be permitted to view them."

There is politeness in his manner but no friendliness. It's as though, as artists, we are all on a similar quest, and therefore should be aware of each other's work. I step back, and with an arm toward the drawings, say, "Please..."

The twins enter the studio and there's not another word spoken, except for quiet exchanges between them in German. As they move slowly around the studio, rather than stare at their emaciated bodies, I return to work at my table. Finally, they appear at my side and the mood in the room has altered.

"I am Hans and this is my sister, Hanna," he says softly. "These drawings, they are..." "Savagely beautiful", she says and looks at me with sad, pale, cobalt blue eyes.

We then move around the studio, talking about specific drawings As the twins talk and gesture, I see that each has deep puncture-wound scars on their hands and feet. Hans sees me stare at the scar on his hand as he's pointing to a drawing.

"Yes", he says, "Come..."

He leads me to a bare wall and leans back, arms out, palms open. Hanna does the same, pressed against him, so that her hands are on top of his and I see that they have rough scars in their palms. She puts her feet over Hans's to reveal more scars.

"What do you see?" Hans asks.

They are in the position they were in when I clandestinely looked into their studio. "A crucifix." I say.

"Precisely", says Hans, "But a reverse crucifix, crucifixion. You see we were saved but our friends, our four closest friends were sacrificed as we all went over the Berlin wall. The guards could not fire bullets fast enough to kill us all, just enough to kill our friends and grant these stigmata wounds to carry out the evidence, and to carry out our work."

They silently look at me. I don't know what to say, and I say, "I don't know what to say."

Hans and Hanna slump down and sit against the wall.

"It's not necessary to say anything," Hanna says with quiet resignation.

They are silent for a few minutes until Hans says, "This Annunciation angel you are making, there is to be a Virgin, yes?"

"Yes, in time. I want someone the exact opposite of this Gabriel, as light and ethereal as this archangel is dark and carnal."

"You are dealing with the scriptures as metaphor as we are." Hanna says.

"Well, I haven't seen your work."

"No, of course. Hans and I would like you to see our performance piece. It's not yet fully realized, but enough so that you can see what it is we're striving for."

As the conversation unfolds, the twins sit against the wall. They are both pale to the point of ghostliness, and from their shoulders to their ankles, their bones seem about to split through their translucent skin. Hans watches me observing them.

"Our intake of calories is only enough to sustain us and we eat only sprouts and grasses that we grow. After our escape and our hospitalization, we decided that life is not to celebrate, but only to bear witness through our art to the Satan in man. This is why we wear no clothes; we believe our stigmata should be seen by all we have contact with."

I look at Hanna, expecting some equally assertive dogma, but she only looks at me briefly with sad eyes and turns away.

Hans continues, "Hanna doesn't feel as strongly as I, but you see only together do we form this crucifixion that is now our legacy, our destiny."

As he speaks, his German accent becomes stronger and verges on the military. After a few moments of silence, Hanna rises and leaves. Hans watches her leave with a frown. We agree on the next morning for me to see them at work and Hans leaves. They each look like something from Auschwitz, and that too seems part of the idea. The word angst has no English equivalent.

The next morning, lying in bed, I'm filled with dread at the idea of watching Hans and Hanna in their studio. When I told Angelika where I was going (our communication is so primitive I had to point to my eyes to convey that I was going to watch the twins at work), she said with sadness, "Bones." A good deal of her English vocabulary is cooking related. Angelika pleads to stay with me after our drawing sessions. There is no sex. How could I have sex with my Archangel Gabriel? Among other things, it would now seem like self-sex. It's hard to believe that Hans and Hanna and Angelika inhabit the same temporal world.

The twins' door is open a few inches and I knock. There's no response. I look in. Hans and Hanna, naked, are on their hands and knees, their heads down low over shallow boxes of bright green grasses. They are eating, or more accurately, they are grazing. Their vertebrae protrude severely in their blue-white skin, lit from the side by the morning sunlight. I realize two truths at once; the twins are possessed and they are dying of starvation. I turn to leave, but Hanna has seen me.

"Oh, Martin, come in."

I turn back to face her. She has raised her head, her long light curls hanging down. She gives me a wan smile, revealing chlorophyll-tinted teeth. She sits back, rubbing her knees and elbows, that are red from the pressure of only bones and skin against the marble floor.

Hans ignores me, keeps on chomping at the grass, his teeth grinding side to side. Hanna watches him sadly, and then looks at me with watery blue eyes. She says nothing. She just looks at me, and in her silence her eyes seem to be pleading with me to see some difference between her and her brother. Finally, Hans sits up and drinks from a water glass at his side. He seems exhausted. There are a couple of minutes of silence, except for Hans's breathing. Hanna has lain down on the floor, her head on her arm.

I look around their studio where they also apparently sleep. There is one bed. The massive cross dominates the room. The beams are roughly hewn, which explains the multitude of small red sores I've noticed on the twins' bodies this morning, splinters from rehearsing their performance.

Hanna says softly from the floor, "I think I'm too tired to do our performance for you, Martin, I'm sorry."

Hans looks at her critically, but it's clear that he too is exhausted. Even in his state of physical depletion, his emotional power fills the room, and with it, his power over his sister.

He looks at me and says with Germanic precision, "We will be ready to show you our work tomorrow morning, can you come back?" I nod.

Hanna's eyes are closed and she seems to be sleeping. I leave. As I wander back through the hallways, I feel certain that if someone doesn't intervene, the twins will die. Or one of them will, the weakest one, and that is Hanna.

That evening, Angelika and I work on drawings for a few hours, and then sip ouzo out on the terrace, leaning against the ancient columns, dazed by the evening Aegean light. I try to explain to her, with more mime than words, what I experienced in the twins' studio that morning. Angelika is serious and sad, clearly understanding what I'm trying to convey. Her sensitivity and island intelligence have become increasingly dear to me. When we get into bed, her myriad fragrances envelope me and I drift off to sleep thinking we've had sex even though we haven't, but it sure smells gloriously like it.

Sometime in the blackness of three or four in the morning, I'm awakened by gentle movement in the bed and soft sobbing. I think that Angelika is dreaming. I reach over, but the gently quaking body I feel next to me is cool and narrow and bony. Hanna has climbed into the bed between Angelika and me. When she feels my hand on her shoulder, she moves against me and pushes her face into my neck and continues to sob softly, her whole body shaking. Her breath is hot and smells sweet, smells of sweet grasses. Angelika curls up against Hanna's back and puts her arm around her. Hanna releases a low moan of gratitude and continues her sobbing. No word is spoken. In time, Hanna's sobs subside and soon she is asleep, lying against me and held by Angelika. It is perfectly still in the room and Angelika too is sleeping. I am awake most of the night, speculating on how to deal with Hans.

I wake early and look over to see Angelika sitting up in bed with Hanna curled up against her. She is being fed creamy yogurt from a bowl. Hanna looks small, leaning against Angelika, with her lips pursed for the small spoonfuls of yogurt she is getting. Angelika gently strokes Hanna's hair and occasionally speaks softly in Greek. As I watch them, I feel a sense of relief. If we can keep Hans from Hanna, her will to survive will win out. Hans, though, is another matter entirely. His will to die seems formidable.

Angelika allows the small amount of yogurt to settle in Hanna's stomach before offering more. Soon Hanna is asleep again. With words and gestures, I convey to Angelika that we must keep Hanna from Hans. After we have taken Hanna, with her zombie-like walk and some carrying, to Angelika's room, I return to the studio and wait for Hans to appear.

When he does, it is midmorning, and he is less worried than angry and suspicious. His German accent is aggressive.

"My sister, you have seen her."

He says this not as a question asked, but as an accusation and I suddenly view him not only as a candidate for suicide, but for homicide. His weapon is his power over his sister.

"Your sister has been taken to Phira, to a doctor, because she is ill, she is starving." His face contorts as he unleashes his fury.

"Who has done this? Our health is our business. The people in this rich man's villa have no right to interfere."

"I have taken her, Hans, early this morning. No one else knows about it."

"You!"

Where the strength for this rage comes from is a mystery; He is as emaciated as his sister. "You have abducted her and I'll have you arrested."

"No, Hanna came to me and asked for help because she wants to live."

"Live! Our art is our life, how dare you interfere!"

He glowers for a few moments, then turns and leaves with a stride as vigorous as Hanna's was feeble.

Hans locks himself in his studio. In the following days, the villa is quiet. I see nothing of Hanna, and little of Angelika other than her brief positive reports on Hanna's progress. She knows she must protect Hanna from Hans, indeed save her from her brother. She locks Hanna in her room during the day and stays with her at night, therefore interrupting our draw-ing sessions. I miss drawing her and am surprised to realize that I also miss her in my life, like I'm missing part of myself. There is no sound from Hans's studio.

It is Good Friday, and Orlando has invited friends to dinner. They are from various parts of Greece, and are archeologists and collectors and cul-tured business people. Late in the evening, we are having coffee on the ter-race. Everyone is quiet and mellow. Penetrating the dark silence surround-ing the villa is the sound of a scrape of wood against stone that seems to come from the topmost crown of the villa. Then a distinct and closer loud thump, and then we all watch a large wood cross with a naked body strapped to it, turning slowly cartwheel style, pass by the terrace on its three-hundred-foot plunge to the Aegean Sea below.

Orlando turns to look at me in horror. He moves quickly to his phone to summon the island police boat. The boat is soon on the scene, its spot-light skimming the water's surface. Everyone watches from above. Finally, the cross is located, face down. As it rotates slowly, rising and falling with the swells, lighted by the spotlight, the effect is one of powerful theater. The cross is finally turned over to reveal loose straps at all the critical points. The velocity and impact have separated Hans from his prop, and foiled his watery ritual on the commemoration day of the crucifixion of Christ.

Late in the evening, Orlando and I talk about the whole affair. He maintains that because the event was Hans's total artistic oeuvre, he would not have allowed himself such a miscalculation.

"He was too intelligent, too motivated, too German for such a mistake. No Martin, I think we've only witnessed the opening scene of Hans's thea-ter piece. On Sunday, Easter Sunday, the day of Resurrection, Hans's body will surface and his macabre work of art will be completed."

I return to my room, and soon after, Angelika appears, her expression a mix of shock and horror.

"Gone, Hanna, gone!"

I am stunned by the thought that we couldn't see the other side of the cross as it dropped past the balcony. Had Hans abducted Hanna from Angelika's room during the long dinner, and strapped her to the back of the cross, before strapping himself to the front? That would explain why he seemed so unconcerned about her whereabouts since she left him. Did he know all along that she was in Angelika's room?

The next day, a sea search is launched for the body of Hans, and perhaps Hanna as well, to no avail. Hans's studio is examined carefully. The cross was launched from the studio balcony, the highest point in the villa. The irregular scrape marks across the floor show a struggle with the weight. Could that weight have been compounded by Hanna's? Angelika's grief is inconsolable. She believes the life of Hanna that has been taken, is the life she saved through careful nurturing.

Sunday, Easter Sunday, dawns to confirm Orlando's theory. The body of Hans is found floating face down, gently rocking against the cliff wall below the villa. There is no sign of Hanna. Two days pass. Still no sign of Hanna. On the third day, she is found. Two young boys have discovered Hanna in a Minoan cave. She is alive but weak, and later tells what happened. After Hans's leap, she had run down the zigzagging foot trail of the cliff, and twenty or thirty feet from the water, in a flash of guilt from her survival, and Hans having gone on without her, she leapt to the sea to go with her twin. When she struck the water, she was knocked unconscious and miraculously washed into the opening of one of the two Minoan caves in the cliff face, used millennia ago when the water level was lower. The slight tide of the sea deposited her on a flat stone shelf protruding from the wall of the cave. She is examined by the island doctor and then returns to Angelika's care. Life at the villa gradually returns to normal.

Late one afternoon, I have a fisherman take me across to Nea Kameni. I climb to the high lip of the volcanic crater and turn slowly to survey the surrounding Aegean, the islands, and the crest of Santorini topped by the whitewashed village. It is perfectly silent. There is no wind. Wisps of smoke rise from the volcano. The sun is low behind a small island to the west, and a few laser streaks of light traverse the distance, glancing off the surface of the sea, off the other islands, off my sunglasses, and I have an intense sense of my mortality, and my insignificance.

Insignificance? From somewhere inside me comes outrage at the notion. "Insignificance?" I shout down at Atlantis, "I am a maker!"

"Maker," what a perfect word I think. I feel a rush of ecstasy, and with it a meditation on the difference between fate and destiny. Fate, just listen to the sound of the word: complete, self-sufficient, conclusive, self-satisfied. But, destiny! Enter into that alive and circular sound, and anything seems possible. I can do anything. I sense a link between this epiphany and my obsession with the Annunciation. I make, therefore I am, and what I make makes me who I am. And further, what I make makes me who I can now become. I feel a giddy sense of euphoria, and am happy to see the trailing V of the blue caique down below, moving toward the Vulcan, to take me back to my studio.

Now that Hanna is safe from Hans and has recovered from her plunge into the sea, Angelika and I have begun to work again on our co-production, the dark delivering archangel Gabriel. She seems more invested in her role than ever, and has begun to press herself against me at odd times for what she says is absorption (my word, not hers, but I know that's what she means) of my intentions, my motivations. It's a peculiar sensation and I can feel undefined energies moving from me to her. It verges on being sexual but it is not. It's as though she's storing up physical passion for later expenditure. Once when she and I are looking at our just completed drawings, drawings that seem to be bursting with message, I say, "These energies need a receiving virgin soon or you're going to implode." Angelika surely cannot understand my words, but she turns to look at me and nods her head emphatically, smiling like a co-conspirator. I add, "But who?", and she looks at me with what can only be described as surprise at my ignorance.

The next day, I'm on a meandering, thoughtful walk when I come upon a stunning apparition. Hanna is sitting, nude, on a stone bench, sunning herself. It is six weeks since her brother's suicide. She is facing me, but her head is tipped down slightly and turned to the right as though studying something while she thinks. She's been reading and one hand is on her open book on the bench beside her. Her hair is luminous in the sun, the roundness of her body modulated by light like a smooth marble sculpture. Her breasts are firm and full, fuller than I would have expected from her former appearance. Her skin, exposed to the Aegean sun, is a mellow gold and the light delicate hairs on her arms and legs are like a patina of silver. She is part wild creature (and the idea thrills me, part Mother of God). I have not moved, but Hanna has heard my breathy announcement to myself, "My Annunciation Virgin." She turns her head to see me staring, but is as calm as before.

"Oh, Martin, I didn't hear you coming."

She smiles her calm beautiful smile and says, "Come sit down, it's lovely here."

She moves her book to make room. I sit and say, "Hanna, you are the Virgin for my Annunciation."

"Yes, Martin, I know. Angelika and I both think I should be, and we were waiting for you to realize it."

I am sitting close to her and the scent of the sun on her skin is stirring. I look carefully at her body. She is aware of this and as she watches my eyes travel from one area to another, tiny goose bumps appear as though my vision is a soft sable brush pulled lightly over the surface of her skin.

I say, "I'm sorry to stare, Hanna, but you are just so remarkable to look at, like a sculptural work of art."

"Look as much as you please, Martin."

She stands then, in front of me, looking down, her eyes intelligent, clear, challenging. Just as Angelika stood before me so I could assess her with my eyes for the role of Archangel Gabriel, Hanna stands looking down at me while I assess her for the role of Virgin Mary. As I shift my eyes, the texture of her skin alters still more, as does her breathing. When I brush her belly with my vision, there is a slight quivering, as though in anticipation of events to come. She puts her hand on her belly, and closes her eyes. Her lips are parted, with tiny beads of perspiration above her sculpted upper lip, where hairs are as light and subtle as Angelika's are black and assertive. I think what a perfect pair this pale Virgin and dark Archangel make. And her nudity strangely makes her chaste and out of reach because there's nothing more that can happen now except sex which is impossible.

Hanna squats on her haunches, watching me intently, still holding my hand, and she leans back, pulling me with her. I just barely manage to keep my balance. Her move is a declaration and she's strong. I stare into her eyes, showing my intense desire. Her eyes are bright with power. She pushes me from her and says "Never."

I roll to my side retrieving my hand.

She turns, her back to me and says, "That is for Gabriel."

What a foolish lapse into my former pattern. Does Hanna now know the role of the Annunciation in my emotional existence? Is this Annunciation going to do me in?

We lie in silence while our breathing calms. Then I rise and holding out my hands say, "Let me help you up, Hanna."

She reaches out and I pull her up. We embrace, carefully, as a truce, and I gently brush from her back and hips bits of sand and gravel pressed into her skin.

"Thank you, Martin."

"The calm before the storm." I sigh to myself.

"Yes." Hanna says.

Back at the villa, I encounter Angelika in the hallway. I greet her with an embrace, and she sniffs me carefully, pulls back and says, "Hanna," and looks carefully into my eyes.

"How do you know the smell of Hanna?" I ask.

"Hanna and I, we know each other." She adds, "What you have done with her?"

"It's all part of the painting. The sooner we start, the better."

She seems so agitated, I add, "I've done nothing with Hanna. Believe me." Then silently, to myself, "The reverse is more to the point."

Two days later, a black-winged, nude Gabriel is before me on the studio floor. She is kneeling before Hanna, as Virgin, who is sitting in a carved Renaissance chair. Hanna wears a blue fabric that is open and spread to each side. Her back is arched, pushing herself out in an arc. Her legs are parted and Angelika kneels between them with her hand curved over the swell of Hanna's belly. Hanna's arms are spread to each side, palms out, displaying her hard-red scars. Angelika looks into Hanna's eyes, her expression one of adoration. Hanna's eyes are downcast and she observes her belly with a small smile.

I have not seen Angelika since our encounter in the hallway and her attitude toward me now seems one of co-conspirator. Hanna seems smug, as though she knows something we don't, which turns out to be true.

The drawings go well. In another week, I'm well into the painting and it unfolds quickly. My process is like a compression of the history of Christian art, my first inclination is a flat Byzantine style of simplification, then a Renaissance rounding of the figures, then back again to a flat, modern style. I want to capture the two individuals combined with the accumulation of the roles they are playing, historically and ecclesiastically, and for me, I realize, personally. The stylistic contradictions are evident as I feel they should be. I become possessed by the process, and am soon at the stage where much of the time I can work without Hanna and Angelika before me. I spend the daylight hours painting, and even late when the clear Aegean light begins to diminish, I'm unable to leave the painting. I sit in front of it sipping ouzo, mesmerized by the change that takes place in the colors as the light fades. The blue of the Virgin's robes becomes progressively lighter as the room gets darker. The swelled abdomen of the Virgin seems levitated by the ethereal silver-blue as though God is presenting this belly for all to admire. As I sit and stare, in a delirium of fatigue and ouzo, I hold out my right hand, my drawing and painting hand, so that the glowing belly of the Virgin seems to be cradled in my spread fingers. The next day the painting will be finished. It is the promise of this thought that finally allows me to sleep, curled up on the floor of my studio at the foot of the Annunciation.

In the morning, Hanna and Angelika are before me. There is a tense silence in the room as I make the final few refinements in the painting. Angelika stares at the belly of Hanna beneath her cupped hand. Hanna's belly is extended with an exaggerated flourish, as though flaunting her womb to the world. Suddenly, Angelika exclaims something in Greek and stares at the belly of the Virgin.

"It move," she says.

She sits back on the floor, and all the Eastern Orthodox intensity of this island peasant imbues her with awe and terror. For her part, Hanna leans back in the chair, stretching herself out, crossing her feet, one scar over the other, one scarred hand lightly touching the scar on her side, the other cradling her protruding belly. Her head is tipped down and to the side, her long curls cover her shoulders. She smiles and moves her hand slowly in a circle over her belly, "Hans," she whispers with Germanic defiance.

Late that night, Angelika comes to my studio. She is frightened and confused. She tells me what Hanna has told her. It takes a long time, even though Angelika's English, tutored by Hanna, has improved daily.

On the night Hans leapt to his death, he convinced Hanna to come back to their studio. (He had known all along that she was in Angelika's room.) He said he wanted to do their performance one more time, that there would be a new element to it.

As Angelika explains what happened, I remember their performance I had clandestinely witnessed from the hallway that first day.

As Hanna, murmuring their strange dirge along with Hans, coiled over on top of him, it was meant to convey a futile attempt at life and living, procreation being the symbol. Hans's impotence, their failed attempt, was the mark of the treachery of the East German regime, and at the realization of his impotence, Hans was to throw Hanna off of him. The night of Hans's leap, his decision to fly his crude cross past the audience on the terrace of the rich man's villa, to plunge into the sea on the commemoration of the crucifixion of Christ, that decision charged him with an inspired virility. So when Hanna lethargically curved her body over his, instead of his tragic, futile display of impotence, Hans gripped her hips, and rigidly erect, plunged into her, spending with a force that shook both their bodies violently. Hanna fainted and fell to the floor. When she regained consciousness, she was shocked at what Hans had done. He was struggling with his huge cross as Hanna ran from the studio. Before she reached Angelika's room, she decided to turn back. Just as she entered the studio, she saw Hans on his cross, balanced on the edge of the balcony, his eyes ablaze. When he went over the side, it was then that Hanna ran down the zigzagging path to the water and in the process decided to leap herself. The rest we know.

And just as it was no accident that Hans's body resurfaced on Easter morning (he had, it was discovered, used weights attached to himself with a system that would release in the prescribed time period). It was no accident that Hanna became pregnant. Hans had made precise notes on Hanna's fertility cycle that made the timing perfect, and perfectly symmetrical. Even so, I could not help but believe that I had something to do with this. But what?

**

Two days later, when I go down for coffee, I find that Hanna has left the villa, and Santorini, and has taken Angelika with her. The Berlin wall had come down the previous week. We had all listened to the news, excited, but had no idea the effect it would have on all of us.

"They have gone off to Leipzig," Orlando tells me, "where Hanna still has family, and there she will have her baby. Do you know what that baby could be?", he asks incredulously.

I say, "I can't even consider the thought," but again I wonder what kind of egregious act I have committed with my obsession.

A month has passed, during which I've made small refinements on the Annunciation. It is powerful, and I'm pleased. When Orlando comes in to view it, he's in a flight of inspiration.

"Martin, may I purchase it?"

"Yes."

He is silent for a moment, and then says, "I'm going to build a separate gallery for the painting, detached from the villa, but close by, a sort of chapel, a secular chapel, but Greek, white stone and blue dome."

The idea pleases me, and I say, "Yes, but there will be more."

"More Annunciations?" Orlando smiles.

"Yes, I think this is just the beginning of my understanding something, yes, there'll be more. I don't know when I'll be doing the others, first I want to return to Italy, to see more Annunciations. There, I sense I'll confirm what I'm beginning to suspect about the meaning to me of these paintings."

Two weeks later, the evening before I'm to leave for Italy, an entourage of white-robed and turbaned Arabs appears at the villa. Orlando knew in advance of their impending arrival, but said nothing to me.

"Martin, you are welcome, of course, to join us for dinner, but I must ask you to ask no questions. In due time, you will know everything."

It's the first time that I've seen this supremely self-confident friend seem even the least bit unnerved and he is clearly more than that tonight.

"I will be a man totally without curiosity," I say.

"Martin, I'm very glad you're here." He smiles and says.

At dinner, Hamm is present as interpreter when needed, and when I hear him refer to His Highness, I know that the Arab with the commanding presence is the Prince whose art collection Hamm once curated. The Prince, middle-aged, plump, and indolent, has about him an air of power over everyone in the room, except for me, and he stares lazily at me a few times trying to assess what role I play in the lives of the players here at the table. Some of the talk has to do with the art collections of the Prince and Orlando, and the Prince, whose English is passable, makes reference to a small Picasso drawing in Orlando's collection. Then he says something, partly in Arabic and partly in English, including the words, 'The boy'. The color has drained from Hamm's face as he asks the new kitchen girl, who is helping to serve us in Angelika's absence, to bring Reginald in. After a few minutes, the girl walks back into the room, and behind her is Reginald, pale and hesitant to enter. Behind him is a blond woman in her thirties whom I've never seen before. She is also in white robes, and her soft blue eyes seem dazed or drugged. The Prince, spotting her, issues a low, authoritative command in Arabic, and she backs out of sight immediately. It is the last I see of her. The Prince motions to Reginald to come to him, and Reginald does. He stands beside the Prince's chair and listens to a long soliloquy in Arabic, occasionally answering back quietly, also in Arabic. As the Prince speaks, he runs his dark, bejeweled hand up Reginald's thigh until it rests on his adolescent hip under his shorts. The room is tense and silent except for the Prince's low droning monologue, and the sound of Orlando's great jowls inhaling and exhaling.

At this moment, the Greek kitchen girl, whom everyone knows is totally enamored of Reginald, enters from the kitchen, staring at the Prince's hand on Reginald's hip. She is carrying a bowl of yogurt meant to embellish the gazpacho that sits bright red in a clear glass bowl in the center of the table. Reaching out as though to place the sour cream next to the gazpacho, she executes a barely believable stumble and sends the bowl of sour cream flying into the gazpacho like a World War II depth charge, sending an explosion of juicy red and green in every direction. It is spectacular, it is Jackson Pollock as counter Mideast terrorist. There is total pandemonium. Orlando stands and orders the kitchen staff to bring in towels and mop up the mess. The Arabs, after some intense exchanges between the Prince and Orlando and Hamm, retreat to their rooms. Orlando and Hamm take Reginald with them to the opposite end of the villa, and I am left in total puzzlement.

On top of all the obvious questions in my mind about the connection between Orlando, Hamm, Reginald, and the Prince, I am haunted by the apparition of the pale blond woman in robes who stood behind Reginald when he was ordered into the dining room. Since I am leaving early in the morning, I suspect it will be a long time before I have any explanation for any of this.

In the morning, just past dawn, Orlando silently appears at my side as I wait for the caique to take me to the ferry on the other side of the island. It is clear that nothing will be said about the previous night.

"I'll be back," is all I say. Orlando nods silently.

As the boat moves away, Orlando waves twice with wide sweeps of a huge blue hanky. It is the blue of the domes of Santorini, and the gesture is the arc of the dome-to-be of the Annunciation chapel. I return Orlando's wave and settle uneasily into my pilgrimage back to Italy and to the Archangels and Virgins that haunt me.

The gentle roll of the ferry urges forth memories just below the surface of my searching mind, searching for a tie between my present painting compulsions and my past pairing compulsions, my frequently failed and futile attempts to bring love, romantic, sensual love into my life. As a savvy friend once said, "If you'd stop pursuing modern Virgin Marys, you might manage to live a normal life." And he was right, a woman had to appear inaccessible to make me want to make her accessible to me "Who do you think you are, God?", a mantra I'm to hear more than once in my odyssey. And of course, Angelika was my alter ego in the painting of Hanna as Madonna, and our lying together, without sex but in our fragrant heated nakedness all those nights, was my means of imbuing her with my passion for an inaccessible Virgin, in this case Hanna. As it turned out, Hans had already done the dirty work, so it was for me, truly an immaculate conception. And I can't help wondering, Did Angelika know all along that she was my surrogate? Does that explain her frequent small smiles of bemusement and her often sudden serious looks into my eyes as though we are each other? So, in my detached and symbolic methodology, with whom did I couple? Hanna or Angelika? Or both? And more to the point, who/what am I in pursuit of in my renewed pilgrimage to Italy?

***

The high whine of an approaching Vespa makes me step quickly back, as the scooter jumps the curb and sprawls across the narrow sidewalk, stopping at the stone wall of the Palazzo Corsini. A girl, having slid clear of the scooter, is on her feet swinging her shoulder bag in ferocious sweeps at a boy who is trying to get the Vespa off his leg. When he gets the scooter upright, with a running hop he is speeding down the sidewalk and out into the busy Roman street. The girl shouts an obscenity after him, and then cries quietly while she leans against the wall, bending to look at her knee.

I walk over to see if she's hurt. "Are you all right?"

"My knee hurts, my jeans have this tear, oh, it's all bloody, that asshole Fabrizio, first he makes me late, then he drives like he's crazy. Now my sister will be gone from here and I must ask her questions for my examination in just two hours."

"Your sister works here at Palazzo Corsini?"

"Yes, she's curator of the gallery."

"Your knee is bleeding, and you should clean this up, your jeans around the rip, I think you slid through some dog..."

"Sheet, si, dog sheet, if there's sheet around, Fabrizio will drag us through it. He is such an imbecile, a rich spoiled imbecile."

"Can you walk okay? You should really go inside and wash off your knee, I have a first aid kit in my pack."

She looks into the courtyard of the palazzo and frowns.

"Oh damn, all the offices will be locked and the bathrooms too. No one will be back until the gallery opens again two hours from now. But there is the botanical garden behind the palazzo and there are fountains there, is it OK that I lean on you? My knee really hurts, this is one huge disaster. In two hours, I have to give this talk at school as part of my exam to graduate, and I have stupidly let this talk with my sister go till the last minute. She knows all about the artist I need to talk about. That stupid fucking Fabrizio, I feel like everything is out of control."

We walk through the shaded and cool courtyard of the palazzo and out into the sunny botanical garden.

The girl asks, "What's your name?"

"Martin, and yours?"

She shrugs her shoulders as though to say, what does it matter, my whole world is coming to an end.

"Paolina."

She is small and delicate with graceful hands and fingers, long straight black hair, pale skin, and surprisingly blue eyes. She's wearing a faded yellow T-shirt, tight jeans, and leather sandals. Her toenails are painted in a rainbow, each a different color.

The botanical garden is enormous and slopes up a hill. We are the only ones here in the midday heat, which is alive with the sounds of buzzing insects and bubbling fountains. Paolina talks about what she was to report on at school.

"The subject of my talk is the humanization that takes place in the Renaissance, and the last part was going to be about the fifteenth century painter Fra Filippo Lippi, because his life and his art were all mixed up together, you see he..."

I say, "I know about Lippi, he absconded with a young nun who he was using as a model for the Virgin Mary."

Paolina says, with wide eyes, "You know about this? Names, places, dates, what the reaction was to this nervy act, all that I was going to ask my sister? This is so exciting, now tell me, what was the name of the young nun he ran off with?"

"Lucrezia Buti."

"That's right, that's the only thing I know. Forgive me for pretending I didn't know her name, but I had to make sure you know what you're talking about and not just making it up. Now, do you know when and where this daring deed took place?"

"Yes, it was in the early fourteen fifties, in Prato, Lucrezia was in the convent of Santa Margherita, and the painting he was making was the Annunciation to be..."

Paolina is grinning. We have come to a low round fountain with water gurgling melodiously from a center grouping of mirthful angels.

"Oh Martin, you're a saint!, no a seraph dropped right from heaven, with everything I need to know, and you've saved me from battle wounds and dog poop, but we need to move fast, I have to be in that dreary institution in just one hour and fifteen minutes to present my talk as though I'd been researching it for a month, now. I've got to rinse out these jeans and wash off this gash on my knee, you said you have a first aid kit?"

Paolina is jumping up and down on one foot in a circle holding onto my shoulder while trying to pull up the leg of her jeans.

"Ow! oh!, I can't pull these up over my knee, they're too tight, I have to take them off, Martin, are we going to be able to do this in time?"

I laugh and say, "We'll do it."

Paolina pauses for a second to give another grin, then proceeds with her rapid-fire monologue.

"Here, I'll get my jeans down far enough so I can sit on the ground and then you can pull them off, it hurts too much to bend my knee."

She hops and wiggles as she struggles to lower her jeans and then sits back abruptly on the grass, resting on her elbows and pushing her feet out toward me.

"Now pull slowly, I'm sorry they stink so much, that asshole Fabrizio, do you have a clean hanky? when we get these off I want to clean my knee before I soak my jeans in this fountain and pollute it forever."

I rinse off Paolina's knee with clean water from the smiling angels, put antiseptic on it, amidst much melodramatic howling, and lightly tape a gauze pad over it. She rinses her jeans, lays them out in the sun, and we have our little tutoring on Fra Filippo Lippi. She sits in front of me on the grass, in her T-shirt and polychromatic toenails, writing furiously as I talk about Lippi, and the frescoes that he painted over a period of years, always with Lucrezia as his Virgin.

Her knee stops bleeding and in high spirits she wiggles into her sun-dried jeans and with her notebook clutched to her chest, she starts down the path to the street for a taxi. She turns back to me.

"Did you enjoy sitting around with me half naked in our little garden of Eden?"

I laugh. "I wasn't half naked."

She laughs and turns and then calls over her shoulder, "Pensione Verado, right? I'll stop by and tell you how we did."

That evening as I'm lost in thought standing by the window in my room, there are three rapid taps on my door. I open it to find Paolina, grinning and holding out a bottle of wine. Behind her is a blond woman looking on, bemused.

"This is for you, Martin, your prize for how well we did in class today. So, Lippi authority Martin, may I present my sister, Lippi authority Vittoria."

Vittoria is in her early thirties and is attractive in a natural way that shows her real efforts in life go into her scholarship, and her looks are quite beside the point. I ask about her work as curator of the gallery, and we talk easily. There is an unspoken sense of there being something very natural about the three of us being together with Filippo Lippi as the common denominator. We go down to sit by the Tiber nearby the hotel looking at a last streak of red in the sky to the west, until Paolina erupts excitedly, "Vittoria, we can take Martin with us next week when we go to Assisi to see Giulia.

She's our sister, Martin, a real sister, in a convent, and there's so much art to look at there. What do you think? Vittoria? Martin?"

Vittoria thinks for a moment, then smiles and agrees, as do I. Paolina claps her hands excitedly.

"Isn't it wonderful what can happen just by serendipity? There, that's a new English word for me."

***

We are in a small rented Fiat on our way north from Rome. I am driving, Vittoria is next to me, and Paolina is in the back seat scrutinizing the food for our trip.

"Mmmm, prosciutto, gorgonzola, tomato, olives, bread, strawberries! Orvieto Classico!, my favorite wine, I'm so excited, I love taking trips. School is over, I have a new love in my life, so Fabrizio can tear around on his Vespa by himself colliding with whatever he wants, that asshole!"

Vittoria turns to look at Paolina and says, "You've dumped Fabrizio? Who's the new boyfriend?"

I can see Paolina in the rear-view mirror, grinning impishly.

"Girlfriend, Vittoria, her name is Sueno, she's Romany, a Gypsy, her name is Spanish and it means dream, and she has dreamy pale gray eyes midst all her dark beauty, and she has this dreamy spicy smell, her hair, her breath, her whole body."

Vittoria has turned to face the windshield again, her face flushed.

After a few moments of silence, Paolina begins again, "Anyway, I'm excited to be on this trip, and aren't you excited, Martin, being jammed into this tiny car with two blue-eyed beauties, and on the way to see a third, the most beautiful of all. I'll gladly take third place, but you have to admit that

I have beautiful toenails, have you noticed? They're all different greens because we're headed for the lush hills of Umbria."

She slumps down so she can stretch her bare legs between the front seats with one foot in front of me and the other in front of Vittoria. Vittoria and I dutifully admire her artistry.

After some silence I ask Vittoria, "How long has Giulia been in Assisi, at the convent?" "Almost twenty years, ever since her brother Nicolò, died. They were twins, eighteen years old when he died, and right after that Giulia went to Assisi to the convent." "How did your brother die?" I ask.

"Giulia and Nicolò were in San Gimignano and there was an accident, a fall, you know how San Gimignano has all those towers. Giulia fell too, and was injured, but Nicolò was killed."

When we arrive in Assisi, Vittoria and Paolina go immediately to see Giulia at the convent, and I settle into a Franciscan monastery where I am welcomed as a guest and as acquaintance of Sister Giulia. The town is filled with idling tour buses and milling groups of tourists following their guides. It all seems like a massive assault on St. Francis. I dread the idea of once again being in the cathedral along with hundreds of tourists. So, I'm delighted to hear from Vittoria that Giulia is allowed to bring single guests to the basilica after it's closed to tours. That night, I'm privileged to see the church with only Giulia

When Vittoria introduces me to Giulia, only for the briefest moment does she allow her eyes to acknowledge mine. Her habit is a beautiful soft gray, with white at her neck and along her face. It is near the anniversary of the death of her brother and her pale eyes are vague from fasting. She is very uncomfortable in my presence.

I say, gently, "Giulia, it's not really necessary for you to do this, I don't mind coming here tomorrow with everyone else."

We are walking toward the church. She slows, and considers what I've said. I sense relief and expect her to accept my offer. She stops and turns to face me fully for the first time. Calmly looking directly into my eyes for an unnerving length of time, she seems in a trance. Then she opens her eyes wider, gently raising her eyebrows as though in mild surprise.

"I'm sorry, when I fast it makes me lightheaded and my thoughts tend to wander." She turns to look at the cathedral doors and then back at me.

"There's something else, Nicolò... I'm sorry, I meant to says there's something else, Martin, that you remind me of Nicolò, my brother who died twenty years ago tomorrow. It's not that you look like him so much, I don't know, it's odd. But, no, I'd like for you to see the frescoes without a crowd around you. Vittoria tells me it's important to you. I'm feeling a little weak, but I'll try to keep up with you as you walk through, and if you have something to ask that I can answer, I'll do my best."

At this, Giulia smiles fully and with a radiance that makes me feel blessed in the most literal sense.

I've been in this cathedral twice before, but both times surrounded by throngs of people. This evening, we're alone in the enormous basilica, where every square centimeter is covered with narratives of the scriptures by the great painters of the thirteenth century, especially Cimabue, and following him, Giotto. The light level is low, with only the late sun penetrating the stained-glass windows with ribbons of color. We are in front of the great but badly damaged Cimabue frescoes of the life of Christ. In addition to the effects of time, and candle smoke, and dirt, a chemical change has taken place. The white lead has been chemically transformed into black lead sulfate, which has reversed all the lights and darks in the images, as though they were photographic negatives of themselves. The gold leaf, however, has remained quite intact. The result is a series of ghostly apparitions, highlighted here and there as we move past, by the shifting reflections of the

gold. We are standing below a huge Crucifixion, with a lamenting Virgin
Mary below. Christ, in Cimabue's signature contrapposto of suspension, is
twice the size of the other figures in the painting.

Giulia begins to speak softly, "This is my least favorite section of frescoes. In fact, I rarely come by to look at these, whereas I come almost every
day to look at the others. This deterioration of the paintings is very disturb-
ing. It's as though everything has been turned around, so deathlike, but not
in the promising spiritual sense. There's a kind of Satanic interference going
on here. When I asked about it, the reason for the change in color, I was told
that the chemical reaction is the result of acid fumes 'exhaled' from the
tombs in the crypt below this transept, you see it only happens in the frescoes directly over the tombs. And what is this acid being exhaled? It is the
fumes of the mortality, the carnality left in the remains below, the souls
having already ascended to their peace above. That's why I call it Satanic,
look what it's done to this Crucifixion, the blood arcing out from the wound
in Christ's side, that blood which becomes a holy element in our Eucharist,
that blood from your side Nicolò..."

Giulia's face is turned three-quarters toward me, but her eyes are still
on the fresco. "...that blood has been turned black by the acid fumes of lust
from below, far below us, and I would never again want to place my hand
in your wound for forgiveness, Nicolò."

Giulia has turned to me now, and while her face is turned up to mine,
her eyes are on my right side, where her upraised hand is a couple of inches
away as though she wants to and doesn't want to touch me. She is breathing
heavily, and her chest is rising and falling, and her breath is hot but sweet.
We stand silently for several moments. She slowly lowers her hand. When
her breathing has calmed, she looks up at me and seems puzzled, then
smiles slightly and enigmatically.

"I'm sorry, fasting this time of year has a very strong effect on me."

As we walk slowly toward the doors of the cathedral to leave, Giulia says in a surprisingly young voice, "Please Nicolò, don't say anything to Vittoria and Paolina."

I turn to look at her, but she keeps walking with her head down. As I watch her, I conclude that she's the most inaccessible attractive female I've ever encountered, with her commitment to the Church, her marriage to Jesus, her robes concealing the slightest hint of her body, and our walking together through this bastion of pure chaste love. And what do I feel? An alarming and torrid desire to make love to her right here on the stone floor of the Basilica of Saint Francis, all to be witnessed by every player in every fresco surrounding us. And in spite of the words I have used, it has little to do with sex.

Giulia pauses to look at me quizzically, pulling her robes tight around her, and I think, are my demons as obvious as Satan's are, in the Last Judgment painting we are walking past?

Vittoria and I are in the car outside the monastery where I am to sleep tonight.

"Martin, I'm worried about Giulia, her stability when she returns to San Gimignano tomorrow. Mother told me that after Nicolò died, Giulia had a nervous breakdown. She was in a hospital, a mental hospital, for almost a year before she entered the convent. She recognized no one in the family and had recurring conversations with dead Nicolò. I have an ominous feeling about her returning to San Gimignano tomorrow."

I look out the car window at the dome of St. Francis Cathedral in the distance, floodlit and surrounded by darkness, and I have a vision of the dome of the Annunciation chapel-to-be on Santorini, bright in the Greek sunlight, and with it a sense that tomorrow will be a day of discovery in my Annunciation odyssey. Giulia is far too intriguing to me. Far too forbidden.

***

The next morning, we are in the small Fiat on our way to San Gimignano. Paolina is next to me, bare feet up on the dash board as she paints her toenails black. Vittoria and Giulia are in the back seat. Giulia is dozing.

"What's the significance of the black, Paolina?"

"Well, it is the twentieth anniversary of Nicolò's death."

"There's San Gimignano ahead, you can see the towers." Vittoria says.

After a few minutes of silence, Vittoria says, "The towers look so ominous, you know they were built so various clans could wage war on each other, and in one case, they killed each other within the same clan."

At this, Giulia abruptly opens her eyes and she stares silently at the towers in the distance. We arrive at San Gimignano in midafternoon, and take Giulia to the small convent in town where she has arranged to spend the night. Vittoria, Paolina and I find a small albergo where we arrange for rooms. We go back to pick up Giulia at the convent, so we can all go to look at the frescoes in the cathedral, which Giulia wanted to see again. Vittoria goes in and returns to the car. "They said Giulia is asleep. I left word we'd be back for her later. I'm relieved she's sleeping, she seemed so exhausted on the way here. If she's going back to where Nicolò died, she's going to need all the strength she can muster."

The three of us walk into the cathedral and move down the central nave.

Paolina is animated, "This is like a giant comic book, all these panels side by side, telling their stories in such a wild and gory way."

Stories of the old and new testaments are painted with the raw zeal of the fourteenth century. In the last judgment, a giant green Satan is gobbling down the damned and expelling them through an anus in the form of a sinister grinning demon. Dozens of other demons are busy at work with pincers, knives, saws, and mallets creating terrible carnage.

"Martin, look up there!"

Vittoria is pointing to a fresco high up under an arch.

"Giulia has been telling me about that painting for the last three days, it's God creating Eve out of Adam's side, from his rib."

Adam is lying on his side, facing into the basilica, surrounded by the flora of Eden. God is blessing Eve as she emerges from a womb-like opening in the side of Adam, stretched to allow her passage.

"What did Giulia say about this painting?" I ask.

"She said over and over how similar Adam and Eve were, with their long blond hair, and how Eve seemed to be emerging from a space she could return to, if she chose, so that they could be together in ways that others cannot."

As Vittoria speaks, she turns to look at me with a frightened expression.

"Martin, let's go back to the convent and check on Giulia, it's been a couple of hours." Paolina and I are waiting for Vittoria, in the car outside the convent.

"Martin, tell me honestly, don't you think Giulia is, you know, a little different? I mean, very different. I mean, really kind of crazy?"

"Well, I think..."

I see Vittoria running from the convent gate, pale and frowning.

"Giulia left the convent an hour ago. The sisters said she was going to meet us at the cathedral, but Martin, we've been at the cathedral for the last hour. What should we do?"

"We'll look for her, the town's small. You and Paolina take the car and Paolina can watch while you drive, I'll walk back to the cathedral and check it out thoroughly, we never moved from the center of the nave while we were there."

Before I go back inside the cathedral, I check the door to the tower alongside. It is locked. I enter the church. The light level is low. I am alone and walk slowly. My footsteps echo in the tall space. I look carefully along the side aisles, the bays, the chapels. The door to the sacristy is open and on a wall near the door, there is a wood cabinet and the door is ajar. I pull it open and inside is a rack of keys, large, old, decorative keys on hooks. At the same time that I see that one hook is keyless, I think again how at times I thought I'd heard echoes of my own footsteps when I stopped at various points in my search of the cathedral. I run from the sacristy, and down the nave to the front door, and around the corner to the tower door. A key is in the lock, and the door is open slightly. I can hear soft sliding steps higher up, and sighs of exertion.

"Giulia, it's me, Martin, please wait for me, I'm coming up." I call out.

The stone steps extend from the walls, each flight turning ninety degrees into the next. I start rapidly climbing the steps. In the center is a straight column of space, running uninterrupted, from the top landing to the stone floor a hundred feet below, with the exception of one protruding iron bar. As I climb, I periodically stop and listen, and when there is silence, I take off my sandals and in bare feet and keeping close to the wall, I continue the rest of the climb in silence. As I approach the top of the tower, I hear Giulia's breathing. When I turn to start up the last flight, I see her sitting primly with her hands on her knees, watching me with a small smile. Her head is uncovered, her short-cropped hair golden.

"I told you I'd get to the top before you."

Giulia says this in a playful and young voice. She is sitting in the center of the step.

Looking toward the deep shaft of space, I say, "Giulia, please move over a little toward the wall so I can sit next to you."

She does and I'm relieved. She then looks straight ahead and after a few moments, with a slightly clouded expression, speaks again in a young voice.

"Did you see the painting?"

"Which painting, Giulia?"

"Our painting, silly."

She puts her hand on mine and squeezes it affectionately. She stares at my bare feet in silence for a moment, and then speaks very quietly in a sad young voice.

"When you took off my sandals and massaged my feet, it felt so good, especially after the long climb up here. But then, I sensed something, something else, and the expression on your face, and I suppose the expression on my face too, don't you think it was the wine, Nicolò? You had been acting so silly, you were so funny, I laughed so hard I thought all the food we'd just eaten was going to come up, remember when you were eating, and you were imitating the huge green Satan in the church fresco chomping down those poor damned mortals and you were saying, wait till you see what happens to them next, to embarrass me, and when you talked about

Adam and Eve being one and the same, two blonds just like us, we who actually look like we're one and the same, and could become one and the same, I thought you were still being a silly clown, Nicolò, just a silly clown..."

Giulia has turned to face me and her eyes are filled with tears.

"And when you said what you wanted to do, and you asked me if I wanted to, and I said yes, because I did want to, and then when you started, my body felt so on fire, I thought to myself, my body is on fire! Then, the Satan in the fresco was not a joke at all, and I was filled with terror, and shame, and guilt, and I looked at you. I looked at you Nicolò, and I saw the devil."

Tears stream down Giulia's cheeks as she sobs. Her body shudders and she turns and hunches over and hugs her knees. We sit in the dark silence until she calms. Then, she speaks in her mature voice.

"I'd like to go down now, Martin."

We stand and start the long descent. Giulia takes my hand and holds it tightly all the way down. When we reach the ground level, Giulia leads me to the center of the floor.

"This is where Nicolò died, Martin. I pushed him you know. After I pushed him, I ran down the stairs. Halfway down, I was overcome with grief and I wanted to die, to go with Nicolò. I jumped. Miraculously, the iron bar that tore open Nicolò's side, saved my life. I had on a small back-pack and the bar hooked a strap. It dislocated my shoulder and the strap tore loose, but it slowed my fall. I landed on Nicolò, which is what probably saved my life." Giulia is calm and articulate as she recites all of this.

"I was knocked unconscious. When I came to, it was light. My whole body was filled with terrible pain. When I became aware of all that had happened, Nicolò was cold and still beneath me, my eyes shifted down to the torn opening in his side, and the image in the cathedral of Eve emerging from Adam filled my mind and I thought, yes, I'll return to where I'll be surrounded by Nicolò's love. It was my intention to crawl inside Nicolò. I did get my hand in, well past my wrist, and that's how I was found when the priest opened the tower door in the morning."

Giulia turns to look at me. She looks down at her nun's habit, clasps the cloth and holds it up and stares at it briefly. She looks down again at the stone floor, and then slowly looks up the shaft of space above. We stand together. I put my arms around her. She stares, unblinking for a full minute. Twenty years of her life, it seems, are being screened in her mind's eye.

When we leave the tower, Giulia returns to the convent in town for the night. Vittoria and Paolina are taking the train back to Rome the next day. I have agreed to drive Giulia back to Assisi on my way to visit some hill towns to look at churches and their frescoes, and more Annunciations. In the hotel that night, Vittoria and Paolina ask what happened in the tower, what Giulia had told me. I am vague because Giulia has asked me to tell her sisters nothing of what transpired. I just say that Giulia is confused and they nod in agreement.

The next morning, we are all sitting outside having coffee in the central piazza of San Gimignano. Giulia, in her soft gray robes, seems in costume, like an actress who has just finished the last act and has not yet been to the dressing room. She looks at the daily life of the town around us with slight alarm, as though this is a new play and she has not yet been given the script.

After we have seen Vittoria and Paolina off at the train station, Giulia and I leave in the Fiat for Assisi. She is quiet as she stares out the window at the passing Tuscan countryside. Because she had asked me to say nothing to Vittoria and Paolina about what happened in the tower yesterday, or twenty years ago, I feel an uncomfortable sense of responsibility for her now. I'm the only one with the true story. In fact, because she slips in and out of the present and the past, I feel I know more than she does about her own life. As a result, I feel a tender tie to her.

After an hour of silence, Giulia speaks softly, "I can't go back to the convent. I was there for the wrong reason for twenty years."

I say nothing.

"And I can't go back to my family in Rome, at least not yet. Can I come with you, Martin, until I decide what to do next?"

She looks over at me with a calm expression that seems to say, after all, I've already told you more intimate truths than I've ever told anyone before. "Yes, you're welcome to come with me." I say.

My mind though is less calm than my voice as I think, what an odd turn in my life, an odd but consequential turn, consequential because I know its connection to my Annunciation odyssey.

"Thank you." She says, and looks out the window at passing vineyards.

***

Giulia and I are standing, side by side, in front of a reproduction of a Sienese Madonna on the wall of my hotel room in Lucca. Giulia's room is next door. We have been traveling for a week, meandering really at her request while she decides what to do next, looking at frescoes, looking at the magical Tuscan landscape, and telling each other about our lives.

She slowly runs her finger down the figure of the Virgin. "Martin, you know I'm a thirty-nine-year-old virgin."

"Then with Nicolò...?"

"That is part of the tragedy. If Nicolò and I had actually been lovers, then maybe the consequences would have been justified, but you see it was only Nicolò's taboo touch that so inflamed me, it was the conflict between my body and my church that resulted in my, my temporary madness, and Nicolò's death."

Giulia turns to see how I've taken what she's said. For the first time since I held her at the base of the tower a week ago, I touch Giulia again. It's involuntary, and an expression of sympathy, and empathy, and now affection for her. I place my hand on the side of her face. A faint blush colors her cheeks and runs down her neck. The texture of her skin changes subtly under my hand. There is a small but audible intake of breath and her lips part to allow it. Her eyes are lowered to look at my hand, and she is frowning slightly. Frowning as though what is occurring is occurring in a language she's unfamiliar with. She reaches for my hand, and I think it's to pull it away, but she keeps it there. Giulia is now studying my eyes for some clues to this language. Then she moves our hands down the side of her neck. I move our hands obliquely over her chin. She moves our hands slowly over her mouth and I feel a slight tremor and warmth in the palm of my hand. She is breathing in quick, short breaths, and she says, "Does it feel like a gift, Nicolò?"

Just as I am about to pull my hand away in alarm, a flash of awareness crosses her face and she says, "Oh Martin..."

When we are still, I consider the matter of being interchangeable with Nicolò. What does Giulia experience when that happens? Does she really believe I'm her brother? Or is it some involuntary expression of denial that he's dead, even after twenty years? Should I stop this, or should I allow it to evolve, believing that in time, the real Martin will replace the phantom Nicolò? Her pale blue eyes are clear as she says, "Dear Martin," and I choose to believe that I will dispel the apparition of Nicolò.

In the middle of the night, I lie in the dark trying to define what has happened to allow me to feel this degree of attachment. Giulia, next to me, is somewhere in between accessible (she has renounced her tie to the church) and inaccessible (she still wears her nun's habit).

Just when it seems she has fallen asleep, she turns to me. I turn to her. We hold tightly to each other and kiss softly. When, after much touching and murmuring, I enter her, I feel tentative tightening. It's as though she is asking, 'What is happening? Who is inside me?' All of a sudden, she pulls me roughly against her, and tightens on me repeatedly. "Nicolò," She murmurs... then, "Oh, Martin... I'm sorry."

The next morning, Giulia is in a playful mood and is perfectly lucid. "After coffee, Martin, I want to buy some clothes."

When we reluctantly leave the hotel to see what the day will bring, I feel the most vulnerable I have ever felt in my life. Giulia has not only evaded my defenses, to become far too important to me, too quickly, she has also provided a competing suitor in the form of a ghost.

In a small clothing shop, Giulia, wearing her gray habit, picks out some skirts and blouses, and asks the sales girl where she can try them on. The poor girl is of course befuddled, but goes along with it all. Each time Giulia emerges from the changing room, she asks my opinion. She looks amazingly like any attractive young Italian woman, even her cropped hair looks very stylish. When she has chosen what she wants, she turns to me and says, "You know, of course I have no money, Martin. I haven't for twenty years."

I pay, and we leave with Giulia wearing a flowered print skirt, a white sleeveless blouse, and summer sandals, carrying one bag with more new clothes and another bag with her gray habit rolled up inside. The sales girl watches from the doorway until our car is out of sight.

We continue on our art observing odyssey, and Giulia echoes my own fascination with the Annunciation.

She says, "Something important has to happen after that dramatic encounter between Gabriel and the Virgin, doesn't it?"

I tell her about my Annunciation painting at Orlando's villa, and about Angelika and Hanna. It's Hanna's story that startles her. She says, "We each have a dead twin." Her confusing me with Nicolò is happening more rarely and I'm beginning to think it was just a result of the shock of reliving her story in the tower at San Gimignano. After two more weeks, we return to Rome.

"Giulia, you look like a person." Paolina says.

"Well I am a person." Giulia laughs.

"I mean you're not a spooky sister anymore." Paolina blushes and says. "You may find I'm a spookier sister than ever." Giulia is having fun.

Vittoria is more reserved, and says, "Giulia, I hope everything works out well for you now."

Their mother, Signora Gheraldi, enters the room, and does not know how to deal with any of this, and ends up treating Giulia like she's a cross between a fallen away nun and a mental patient, home for a visit. Giulia is unfazed, and says, "I guess I'm a spooky sister and a spooky daughter."

No one knows how to respond.

I collect my mail from the Amex office, and there's a postcard from Santorini. On one side is a primitive Gothic Archangel Gabriel and on the other, in a clumsy scrawl, with a kitchen stain or two, are the words, "My wings they are out and waiting. Bring home a new Virgin."

I show Giulia the message from Angelika, and she says, in a tone less flippant than in her attitude toward her family, "That would be me, wouldn't it Martin?"

"Yes, that would be you."

***

In another week, Giulia and I are in the blue caique heading toward the villa landing dock.

Giulia is apprehensive. "Martin, I can feel so much here, recent history, ancient history, impending history. What we do in life becomes immediate history, doesn't it? This seems like a place where stories are left behind. I feel surrounded by stories. And we will leave our story here, too."

When we step off the fishing boat onto the dock, we can hear the elevator approaching. Inside the cage, Angelika is peering out, giving us her island-drowning smile. She is very welcoming of Giulia and then turns to me.

"Hello, Annunciationist," she says.

"Hello, Angelika. There's no such word, you know. Have you learned so much English that you have to start making up new words?"

Angelika drowns her moles once again and says, "It is good word, Hanna and I make it up together."

"Hanna? How is Hanna, where is Hanna?"

"Hanna is coming here, and also Hans."

"Hans?"

"You see soon."

Angelika turns to Giulia. "You are virgin?" Giulia looks puzzled.

"She means with a capitol V," I say to Giulia.

"Oh," Giulia laughs again, then adds, "Maybe."

"We see." Angelika says. Then she comes to me and for the first time kisses me on the mouth, briefly but with energy. Then she walks to Giulia and does the same, more fervently. Giulia is caught off guard. She says, "I..."

But Angelika interrupts, "Holy Virgin, Archangel Gabriel, and Annunciationist. We are all here."

Walking toward the elevator behind Angelika, Giulia whispers to me, "Were you and Angelika intimate?"

"No, that's the first time we've ever kissed." Giulia seems perplexed, but not seriously so.

As we walk from the elevator platform up the path to the villa, the doorway ahead is filled with the great mass of Orlando smiling warmly. He is his usual gracious self in welcoming Giulia and makes her feel her appearance at the villa is the highlight of the season for him. He and I embrace affectionately. As we all walk through the hallways of the villa, Orlando answers questions from Giulia about various works of art. When we pass the dining room, looking in I remember the last scene I witnessed there, the night before I left for Italy. I also realize that I've seen no sign of Hamm, or Reginald. As Giulia and Angelika walk ahead toward my room, I turn to Orlando and ask about them. Orlando's ebullience fades quickly.

"Reginald, alas, is in an Arab prison, and Hamm is there to plead his case. It's complicated..."

He waits until Giulia and Angelika are well ahead of us before he continues.

"The British Consulate is involved because Reginald, as Hamm's adopted son, is a British subject, and the Swedish Consulate is involved because, well, I'll explain that in a moment."

I'm stunned, and I ask, "Reginald in prison? Whatever for?"

"He stabbed the Prince in his private parts, not a serious wound, but an egregious one symbolically. It's a hazy story and everyone has a different version. Reginald says the Prince, who is known to partake of bizarre combinations of drugs, attempted to castrate him, turn him into the harem eunuch, and in the struggle to protect himself, the Prince was stabbed. That's the version I believe. The Prince maintains that Reginald's attack was unprovoked, was a calculated assault as the result of Reginald's discovery that the pale blond beauty in the harem, the Prince's favorite, is in fact Reginald's mother. That's the reason the Swedish Consulate is involved. Henrietta, Reginald's mother, the blond woman who had appeared briefly behind Reginald the night of the dinner with the Prince, was a young Swedish girl when she originally came to the Mideast as an au pair for a wealthy Prince in one of the Emirates."

As Orlando tells his story, I sense missing pieces and I ask directly, "Orlando, how are you connected to all this? Why did Hamm and Reginald end up here in the first place? And in such a shroud of mystery, I might add?"

We are interrupted by Giulia, who is coming back down the hallway, showing such pleasure in being at the villa, that I have to break off my intriguing conversation with Orlando.

"Later, over gin, my friend, I'll finish my tale." He says.

As Giulia approaches she says, "Thank you for having me here, Orlando."

Orlando beams and says, "It's my pleasure, my dear, you may stay here forever." We all laugh, and little do we know.

That evening, after dinner on the main dining terrace, Giulia says, "I'm exhausted, I'm going to turn in. You two can catch up on all your news."

Orlando and I sit in silence for a while, sipping brandy, and after telling me how pleased he is with Giulia's presence, he stares out over the Aegean Sea, with its millennia of Greek Gods, Greek myths, and Greek tragedies. Then he continues his earlier story.

"I had a son, Martin. He was the consequence of a youthful encounter that seemed at the time of small importance, until the fact of the boy's imminent arrival in the world was announced to me. It was a complicated situation, and the details are of little importance now. The woman was very intelligent, but extremely unstable, which made it impossible for us to be together.

Eventually she disappeared, only to request money periodically for herself and the boy, and I always complied. This went on for almost two decades. In the meantime, I made my fortune and proceeded to acquire my art collection. Over the years, my son came to the villa a few times. He didn't seem to know what he wanted. It was always very tense, and he would leave quickly. Sadly, I felt little connection to him, and eventually I ceased to hear from him.

"Then, fourteen years ago, I received here, at the villa, a visitor from Sweden. He was an older man, a Lutheran minister. He brought with him the memory of a conversation he had with the mother of my son, who was now dead. She apparently had wanted me to know the fate of our son.

"He told me the story of my son, who had died fifteen years earlier. It seems he was a terror to the world, a drug dealer and an addict. The minister then told me the story of my son's death. He said that at the end of a drug-infused religious odyssey, in which he believed himself to be God, he announced that he would bequeath to the world a savior. He was in the Arab Emirates at the time, and encountered a seventeen-year-old Swedish governess to the children in the palace of the Prince, our Prince, for whom he had been supplying heroin. Exactly when and how he managed it is not known, except by the girl herself, but he impregnated her, as an act of God, he said, and then he killed himself. How he killed himself, Martin, is noteworthy.

"After his sexual liaison with the girl, he walked from her room and through the royal parlor of the Prince's family, saying as he went, I arrived as Gabriel and I will leave as Gabriel, and at this he raised his arms wing-like, and leapt out of the window to a stone courtyard sixty feet below."

There is a silence as Orlando and I look out at the descending dark of the Greek night.

Then he turns to face me and says, "The Prince, a nasty piece of work, as you witnessed at the dinner the night before you left for Italy, has used Reginald's mother as a hostage. At some point, he acquired the information that the man who impregnated his favorite mistress, was in fact my son, who subsequently produced an heir, Reginald (who is my grandson) and who stabbed the Prince in his privates. And because the court system of his small fiefdom is interchangeable with the royal family... well, Martin my boy, you can see it's all a bit of a mess."

I tell Orlando that I'm overwhelmed with his story but I'm too exhausted to say anything, that I want to think about it and talk again. He understands. I leave the balcony that's filled with Orlando's alarming past, and climb into my bed, occupied in my mind by my sweetly disarming present, my Madonna.

***

Two days later, in my studio, Angelika is before me in profile, on one knee, her right hand thrust out. She wears a black fabric wrapped around her and tied at the waist. Her rigid black wings are extended behind her. In front of her is Giulia, facing me but with her head turned toward Angelika, her eyes slyly lowered. She is wrapped in a blue fabric, which she clutches tightly just below her breast. I am drawing fervently on a large sheet of paper. The only sound in the room comes from the graphite marks I make on the paper before me. My second Annunciation is underway, and we work on it every day. I feel compelled to make this image, and Angelika and Giulia have no choice but to play their parts to the end.

Three weeks later, Angelika, her wings erect, is looking intensely into Giulia's eyes. She is very serious, with a slight frown, and her lips are partly open and pushed forward as though delivering Gabriel's message with compelling conviction. Giulia's eyes are wide, as though with awareness of a change within her. I am before them, painting on a large stretched canvas. Giulia has suddenly dropped her head to stare into her lap, and has pressed a hand between her thighs. She slowly raises her head. Her cheeks are pale, her eyes half-closed. Her lips are parted as though she is about to cry out, and she faints, falling into Angelika's arms. I carry Giulia to a couch where she lies pale and subdued. Angelika kneels at her side, still wearing her wings, and lays her head close to Giulia's. As Angelika gently strokes Giulia's hair, she says something repeatedly in Greek. Giulia speaks softly as though to herself, "It's so strange, I am throbbing and aflame."

She opens her eyes wide and stares at Angelika and me, as though she doesn't know where she is, then closes her eyes as though exhausted. Soon

Giulia and Angelika are sleeping. Giulia is on her back. Angelika leans across her, her face pushed against Giulia's breast and her shiny black hair splayed out across the blue fabric like a splatter of drawing ink. Her black wings spread behind her as though she had, just moments before, dropped from above.

***

A week later, Giulia and I are walking, hand in hand.

"Your powers as an artist, Martin, they have come to fruition." She says. "Fruition? You mean because our Annunciation is now complete?"

"No, Martin, I mean I am pregnant."

I hold Giulia. I am awed by her words.

We are standing together quietly, looking out at the late Aegean light. Giulia is staring down at her belly.

"Do you think you're God now, Nicolò?" She whispers.

I am stunned by her words. Every ounce of fear of loss I've felt since meeting Giulia fills my soul. I know now that my penchant to declare a woman forbidden and taboo has been my protection against loss.

"Nicolò dear, give me your hand, it's so lovely here." Giulia is speaking, the next day, in a young voice. We are alone in the low, chapel-like space beneath the branches of the olive trees.

She is as lovely as ever. Her expression is calm, her brilliant blue eyes showing not the slightest sign that I am Martin, not Nicolò. I reach to put my hand gently on her cheek, but she steps back and says, "No, Nicolò, that only brings trouble." She is wearing the soft gray habit of the Order of Poor Clares of Assisi, as she has since the birth of her son, as soon as she named him Nicolò. She attempted to return to the convent in Assisi, and was puzzled when that was denied her. She has found an old stone storage building some distance behind the villa, which she refers to as the convent, where she now lives. Ever-accommodating Orlando had it cleaned out and whitewashed, even though that saddened him deeply. Having the 'convent' to retreat to seems to have hastened Giulia's decline. In her mind, it's like being in Assisi all over again. I miss her terribly, and can't help but believe that somewhere inside her, there is still my Giulia. But in fact, she will never emerge again. What we have in common now is that we each have our own apparition, Giulia has the ghost of Nicolò, and I have the ghost of Giulia. Too disheartening to dwell on.

Hanna has returned from Germany, and brought her child with her. No one has yet seen her little boy, whom she has named Hans. When they arrived, he was all bundled up, and even now Hanna and the boy are rarely seen, and when they are, usually from a distance, the child wears a little hooded cap. and has a limp. They are living in a private corner of the second floor of Giulia's convent. Also living there are Giulia's sister, Paolina, her Gypsy girlfriend Sueno, and Angelika. As a result, Giulia's son Nicolò has a plethora of surrogate mothers, and is thriving.

One afternoon, I am on an introspective wander along a path some distance from the villa, and I come upon the small clearing and stone bench where I saw Hanna, nude and sculpture-like, sunning herself over two years ago. The memory of that and thoughts of all that has happened since, fill me with fatigue, and I find a shady place nearby to nap, always my gratifying escape.

I awaken to a soft affectionate female voice, a German-accented voice. "Ah, little Hans, you need to go?"

I slowly turn my head, and through the rosemary and lavender surrounding me, I see Hanna sitting on the bench, in the sun, nude and sculptural, holding the hand of a little naked child whose pelvis is pushed forward, as though to urinate. But there is no stream arcing out, instead, urine gurgles forth from a small cleft and runs down the inside of first one leg and then the other, smaller and misshapen leg.

The child giggles.

Hanna says sternly, "Hans, you must learn to pee like a little man."

This little girl I am observing with Hanna has rich blond curls and huge blue eyes that she repeatedly turns to her mother, as though expecting Hanna to see something inside, some truth to correct this misunderstanding of how to pee. The child's mouth is slightly agape, suspending a ribbon of drool, the only sign that all is not right with this offspring of siblings.

I'm certain this is a dream, and I close my eyes again hoping that when I awaken, Hanna and her little girl boy will be gone. When I do awaken, the bench is empty, and when I walk to it, I see a moisture stain down one side and bending down to smell it, I confirm that it is indeed urine.

Orlando and I are walking behind the villa. Just on the other side of the olive grove, on an outcrop of rock ledge with nothing on three sides but dazzling expanse of sea, islands, and sky, is the just completed Annunciation chapel. Orlando has forbidden that I see the building and its installation until it was finished.

It is a round white structure, with a blue dome that seems suspended above the walls. Once we are inside, I see that the sense of suspension comes from a circular clerestory that floods the interior with indirect sunlight. There are also tall, narrow, arched windows in between the walls reserved for the paintings. The two Annunciations are in place. On the left is the first painting, with Angelika as Gabriel and Hanna as Virgin. The recently completed Annunciation, again with Angelika as Archangel and now Giulia as Virgin, fills the second wall of the small building. The paintings are perfectly hung in the elegantly proportioned gallery. I am startled by their power, as though they have come from the hand of another painter and I'm seeing them for the first time.

Orlando is silent, he knows how good the work looks.

Then I look at the remaining bare wall, the space for a third Annunciation, and it is there, in two dark, arched panels, side by side. In the left panel is a dark, dark-robed Archangel. In the right panel is a dark, white-robed Virgin. The faces are identical. It is the fact of the Gabriel and the Virgin being one and the same that startles me even more than seeing the vision itself. What could this mean?

They disappear in seconds. I step quickly to the wall, putting a hand where each of the two panels were. I drop to my knees and press my face against the cool stone wall as though to try and make peace with the third Annunciation before it is even begun. All of my dreaded fears of loss that have haunted me for a lifetime seem embodied in the dual image that came and went so effortlessly. Now, it's as though I fear not only the loss of another, but the loss of myself.

Orlando is alarmed. He has never seen me not in control. As is usually the case, those most in need of control are those most fearful without it. And that is what I feel now, fear of what I don't know, fear of what seems like a years ago Hans-like theater piece in which I am only one player. I feel a sudden empathy with Hans. I can imagine myself, with these Annunciation panels strapped to me, like some prototype Da Vinci flying machine, cascading down the face of the cliff on my way to the Aegean.

Is this really all about me, pleading for a connection, a consummation, I will never have? Finally, I stand. Orlando has his hand sympathetically on my shoulder.

I say, "I think I'm just exhausted, I should be able to look at this blank wall and feel inspiration, not..."

I decide not to tell Orlando what I've just seen on the wall.

We retreat to the terrace of the villa, where I enjoy the solace that the company of Orlando always provides, as we sip our ouzo and watch the light diminish around the islands to the west, which are suspended in the usual warm blue of the sea and the cool blue of the sky. Orlando is a solace because he believes in art as much as I, and while he's an accomplished connoisseur, a man with a flawless eye, who has worked hard to gain entry into the realm of art, he hasn't tread in the terrible arena of the making of art, and therefore has a stability that complements my own demons. Like most friends who complement each other, Orlando and I are at ease with long periods of silence as we sit together. This calm seems like a hard-earned recess between my recent Annunciation obsessions (and their consequences) and the Annunciation to come, whose consequences I can't imagine.

***

Two weeks later, unexpected visitors appear at the villa. The senior priest of Santorini, a friend of Orlando's, arrives with two nuns from Romania. One is the Mother Superior of an Eastern Orthodox Order. The other is a young nun who has accompanied her as aid and translator. They have come to appeal to Orlando for funds to restore the famous painted monasteries of Bucovina, which did not fare well under the regime of the late communist dictator, Nicolae Ceaușescu.

The nuns are dressed in green-black habits, and squarish wimples. Both are short and compact, and have dark complexions. The Mother Superior seems to be in her eighties, and her young aid in her early twenties. The expressions of each are severe and unsmiling. They are uncomfortable in the presence of all this wealth, but probably would be uneasy anywhere other than in their cloistered monasteries.

But there is a crisis in Bucovina, and they are forced to appeal outside their country for help. They have brought photographs of the monasteries to show Orlando both the beauty and the damage of their painted churches. Orlando has invited me to sit in, because the buildings are strikingly beautiful.

This order of the Eastern Church is in a remote northeast corner of Romania, and there are several monasteries within twenty or thirty kilometers of each other. They were built in the fifteenth and sixteenth centuries and the style of each is identical. The buildings originally housed monks and priests, but now only nuns occupy them. They are called the painted monasteries because the churches themselves were too small to accommodate the multitudes of peasants who came for mass, so the exterior of the churches were painted, literally covered with Byzantine-style frescoes of saints and scenes from the scriptures. The quality of the painting is extraordinary.

The young nun holds out the photos, with her squarish competent hands, pointing now and then to areas of severe damage to the frescoes.

"You see here", she says, "the stucco it break away and take bits of paint and gold leaf, this because of leak in roof..."

She raises her head for the first time to look directly at Orlando, who is seated next to me, and then at me. She seems frightened by her role here, and she has moist eyes from the tragedy of the disintegration of this holy art. But also I realize, as I observe her striking animal beauty, there is an element of tragedy in the face of this very young nun that goes far beyond damaged frescoes. As I see this, my eyes narrow involuntarily as is my habit when scrutinizing art. She sees this and in response, narrows her own dark eyes and hesitates a microsecond in her words. She recovers at once, and no one else has noticed. She does not, however, look at me again in the course of her appeal.

In the end, Orlando agrees to fund the restoration of the frescoes, and the repairs to all the churches to protect the frescoes in the future. The Mother Superior smiles slightly for the first time as she thanks God for Orlando's generosity. The young nun remains sober in expression.

They stay for lunch during which the young nun translates questions and answers about present day Romania, but in the process does not look at me again. Everyone retires for an afternoon siesta to escape the midday heat. The nuns are leaving at the end of the day, and the Mother Superior is tired and needs to rest. They are provided rooms in the eastern most wing of the villa, which is quite separate.

All is still in the villa, but the brief eye contact with the young nun has left me oddly agitated and I know that sleep is unlikely. I walk to the olive grove and through it on the path that leads to the Annunciation chapel. As the building comes into view I see at the doorway a movement of green-black fabric. I walk quickly and quietly, circling the round building to approach it from the rear. Below one of the narrow-arched windows, I squat and cautiously peer inside.

The young nun is standing in the center of the room, looking first at one Annunciation and then the other. Her lips are slightly parted and she seems stunned by the images. After a few moments she seems to relax and her lips move as though she's speaking. Then she tilts her head to one side and raises her eyebrows. She moves her right-hand part way forward in a tentative Gabriel gesture, then pulls it quickly back and looks toward the closed door. She turns again to look at the paintings and smiling slightly she goes down on one knee and slowly moves her right hand forward. She stands again and looks toward the door, then walks to it and looks outside in all directions. She moves back in front of the paintings, and as she looks from player to player, she steps backward, making a number of slight hand movements mimicking the archangels and Virgins. She stops when her back is against the wall, that blank wall for the third and last Annunciation. She bites lightly at her lip while she contemplates all the players before her. Then she reaches up and pulls her wimple from her head, dropping it behind her. Her hair is cropped short and is thick and black as ink. I can, for the first time, see her clearly, and while her face is wide, her features are fine and her cheekbones are high and tinged with delicate pink. Her eyes are like coal, but they have the brightness of keen intelligence. Her mouth is small and youthful.

With a decisive gesture she runs her fingers back through her hair, then turning to the left, drops to one knee and thrusts out her right arm with authority, her wide hand assuming the Gabriel gesture of pronouncement. She dips her chin down and stares with conviction at the absent Virgin. She opens her lips a little as though to give verbal supplement to her hand message. She stays in that position for several moments, quivering slightly with the effort to hold perfectly still.

Then she stands, takes two steps to place herself in the position of the Virgin who would have just received the word from Gabriel. She sits back against the wall, her body facing forward, but her head turned three-quarters toward the absent archangel, and her eyes with lids half-lowered turned the rest of the way. Her right hand clutches her habit just below her breast, and her left hand is cupped over her thigh, as was true with Hanna and Giulia.

Again, she quivers slightly with the effort to hold perfectly still, as though for the painter out front, the painter whom she now turns her eyes toward, as though for approval. But there is no painter out front, there is just the upper half of my own face in the window on the opposite wall, which this young girl's eyes light upon. There is the briefest squint, and then an explosion of black fabric as she grabs her wimple, leaps to her feet, and holding up the hem of her habit, revealing high-topped black shoes that clamber across the marble floor and out the door with astonishing speed.

I run around the building in time to see her disappear into the olive grove, black fabric flapping like a young raven. I stop, knowing that to pursue her would cause her agony. I decide to stay away from the villa until they leave, in spite of my fascination with what I've witnessed. And what have I witnessed? I have the unnerving sensation that I have witnessed myself as giver, as receiver, as creator. I don't know what it means and I feel very vulnerable.

The next day I walk back into the Annunciation museum and look at the blank wall, and then it strikes me. What I saw yesterday, I was not seeing for the first time. This young nun was the Gabriel and the Virgin I saw as a fleeting apparition the first day I walked into the new chapel, and with it experienced my own longing.

I tell Orlando what I witnessed with the young nun yesterday.

"Well my friend", he says lightly, "that is testimony to the power of those images."

But when I begin to question him about the precise location of these monasteries, and specifically which one the young nun came from, his expression changes and he says, "Martin, forgive me, but you're as wild-eyed as you were when you made the first two Annunciations. Surely you're not planning on..."

But he stops and stares at me because it is clear that, yes, I am planning on going to Bucovina to find the young nun and somehow arrange to paint her. Finally, Orlando walks over, puts his hand on my shoulder, and says, "Martin, it's mad."

I look at him and say, "You're right, it is a form of madness."

The next day, after going to see his friend the priest, he gives me a map pinpointing the location of the monasteries, but says there's no way of knowing which one cloisters the young nun.

***

I am in a temperamental, rented Dacia, driving east to Bucovina, sharing a winding road with horse-drawn carts, and loosely herded sheep. This will be a long drive, five hundred miles east of Budapest, where my train journey across Austria and into Hungary ended, and where I rented this car for the drive into Romania.

I am struck by the contrast between the unchanged Romania, and the destruction wrought within the last fifty years by the country's dictator. In this, the northern part of the country, his obsession with modernization is seen only occasionally and that makes it all the more startling. After a day of driving through these Transylvanian Alps, so stunning in their pristine, dramatic beauty, I come upon the Hotel Dracula. This enormous quasi-castle, built crudely of stone with a red and black Dracula theme throughout, is perched high, with a view across unspoiled valleys and mountain peaks. It was built to accommodate the anticipated hordes of tourists who would flock to admire what the dictator believed to be his beautiful and modern country. In other parts of the country, he had totally razed centuries-old towns and villages and moved the populace to concrete block housing, now collapsing from abuse and resentment.

I am exhausted and decide to spend the night in this 'castle'. There are a hundred rooms but only a few seem occupied. An old bus filled with Gypsies and a half-dozen or so of their dogs is in the parking lot, and these people begin to wander the hallways of the hotel, using bathrooms and harassing the management. The dogs are running through the hallways, barking excitedly and relieving themselves here and there on the red Dracula carpet. I'm cornered in a corridor by a group of dark and dark-eyed children. They converge on me, shouting wildly, and I feel little hands emptying my pockets of the change they find.

In the morning, I have tea and bread early. I am anxious to be on my way east. As I drive down the hill from the hotel, I encounter what seems to be a wedding party walking up toward the hotel. There is a white clad bride and a groom in black. They are surrounded by about fifty or sixty peasants spread across the road so that I have to stop to let them pass. The bride and groom are pink-cheeked young farm peasants, flushed from wine and happiness and the walk up the hill. As the party passes me, an older peasant with a wine bottle gestures for me to open my window for a drink. He seems too mischievous, so I decline, and he pours some wine on my side window with a hard-eyed stare. They continue up the hill and I continue down.

I wind through the Alps and descend into valleys before reaching the Carpathian Mountains. Passing through villages, the people I see seem unaware of lives other than their own. When I reach Bucovina, which contains the monasteries within a small radius, I devise my plan. I will visit each, quietly and with no questions. I will just keep looking, and returning until I find her, regardless of how long I have to stay in these mountains.

As I continue on the narrow road, I see coming toward me on foot, a Romanian herder, tall and sinewy, and dressed in sheepskin, surrounded by loose sheep filling the road so that I have to stop. As he passes the car on my side, he stares hard at me, shouts something and slaps the fender three times with the palm of his hand so hard the car shakes.

The bell at Voroneţ, the first monastery I visit, is rung on the hour. It is loud and from another time. The same bell used to bring forth the faithful four centuries ago. The sound which enters my ears and the reverberation that travels up from the stone path I stand on, meet near my heart and fill me with apprehension. The smell of damp earth and wet stone is timeless, and the only sound, once the echoes of the bell subside, is the wind blowing down from the surrounding hills into the monastery grounds, contained and protected by the massive stone walls.

These high walls, built four hundred years ago to keep out marauding armies, seem to sense my role as intruder, but I am soon allowed in by a middle-age nun, for a small amount of Romanian lei. Her attitude is one of cool tolerance. She doesn't look into my eyes and I sense that her preference would be that no one from the outside enters, but the church relies on these fees. Her robes are the exact green-black of the nuns who came to the villa, and her complexion is identical. The nuns who occupy this monastery live in low-stone buildings against the walls on the periphery of the grounds. These buildings are not to be approached, but I am allowed around the rest of the grounds and inside the church. My first view of the church brings forth a gasp. The structure is long and narrow and the end I'm facing is rounded. The roof sweeps down and extends out in a sail-like curve built to shelter the peasants from the weather while they stand outside for the mass. The architecture seems modern, and timeless, it could have been done by Le Corbusier, the designer of the chapel at Ron champ in France, had he worked in the mid-sixteenth century rather than the mid-twentieth, and had he been joined by an army of obsessed fresco painters.

As I walk the grounds, I begin to see a few more nuns, and I'm surprised to see how young they are, in their twenties and thirties. They are going about their daily chores, hauling water from a well, tending gardens, washing vegetables, cutting weeds with a scythe along the wall. Everything is perfectly maintained and these young nuns seem in total harmony with their world. There is only occasional soft conversation, but it doesn't seem guarded or intentionally spare. It seems part of the same grace of simplicity that is the character of everything here.

As subtly as I can, I maneuver my way around the grounds to get as close a look as possible at the nuns who are outside. From a distance, they all look like her, small, slightly stocky in build, squarish face, olive skin, dark eyes, but none is she.

It rains steadily as I drive to other monasteries, Moduvița, Humor, and finally Sucevița. At Modovița and Humor, I have the same experience as at Voroneț. The grounds are enclosed by stone walls, the churches overwhelmingly beautiful, and the nuns in their green-black robes and wimples, seeming to look alike, are all coolly tolerant of me, but she is not among them.

When I reach the tiny town of Sucevița, it is near dusk and raining still. I'll wait till morning to see this monastery that is at the edge of town. The Hotel Sucevița is one more monument in a state of disintegration. The room I am given, one of only two occupied out of perhaps fifty or sixty, has a broken window with glass still on the floor. I take it gratefully however, because there is no alternative.

When I go down to the dining room, I walk through what was a large carpeted reception hall, now dark and emptied of furniture and permeated with the stench of urine, animal or human, or both. While the rest of the hotel is tomb-like, the dining room is bustling. It is filled with people from the village, and farm peasants, and smoke, and shouts. The floor is strewn with broken glass, that everyone, including the waitress ignores. I sit against a wall, so that no surprise will occur behind me.

The waitress comes calmly over, in spite of the frenzy in the room, and says something in Romanian.

I smile, shake my head and say, "American" gesturing toward myself.

"Essen?", she asks, and the limited German between us gets me my meal. She even smiles slightly at a misunderstanding we have, and I am immediately more comfortable here, in this world more foreign than any I have experienced. By the time I've had a few sips of wine, a dense red that's slightly sweet in a gratifying way, I begin to see all that's happening in this room, not as a menace, but simply as the way things are here. My dinner is lamb and potatoes, and the ubiquitous salad of pickled vegetables, and is surprisingly good. It has been cooked by the waitress. I later realize that this carnival of a place is the work of this one woman. She is in her late thirties I would say, and is handsome in a country way, her face ruddy, with high cheekbones, dark expressive eyes, her mouth full and sculpted, her teeth are fine and white when revealed by her judiciously offered smiles, rewards for my careful efforts to charm her. She knows I am making these efforts, and I suspect that it's only the effort she finds charming midst this male bastion, loudly shouting at each other comments on who knows what. In any event, they ignore her, except to express their food and drink needs.

In a couple of hours, leaning back against the wall, I'm sipping a Romanian brandy that's not smooth, but is tastier by the sip. The din from the peasants has lowered to slow guttural exchanges that seem to be how they might speak to their farm animals when imploring them to move along. In spite of the thick, smoky air and shattered glass, a feeling of well-being has infused my tired mind.

It is still raining outside and black and cold, but I am in a chrysalis of crude exotica. I feel a tie to all these people, simply because we are all here, so far from anything familiar to me. And in the morning, I will enter the gate of the monastery, where I feel certain I will find her.

In the morning, I wake to a steady blowing rain, occasionally gusting through the broken window. Stepping carefully around the glass, and looking out the window, I see what were built as quaint individual guest bungalows. These are a long row of small alpine-style log structures with steep roofs. Some of the doors are open and pigs wander in and out, nosing through the hotel garbage that seems to have been freshly deposited. One more gift from the peasants to the ghost of the dictator. The wit and irony of this immediately raises my spirits.

In the dining room all is quiet, the floor still strewn with broken glass, dishes still on tables, and the smell of last night's haze still in the air. A round, pink-cheeked peasant girl is unenthusiastically trying to bring some order to the chaos. The waitress appears, and points to the one cleared table by the window, and soon brings coffee and bread and preserves, all of which are delicious.

When I pay to leave, she looks at me with such concern at my presence here, in this bleak pocket of the world, that I can only shrug my shoulders as though to say, if we spoke the same language and I told you my story, you'd be even more concerned. I go out the door wearing her worry like a cape wrapped around me against the cold damp morning.

As was true of the others, the grounds and church of this monastery are surrounded by high stone walls. There is a bell at the heavy oak gate, and I pull on the thick rope that rings it. I am surprised to find this gate closed, the other monasteries were at least accessible, if not welcoming. After a few minutes, the door opens a crack, and one more archetypal Bucovinian nun peers out at me. I go through my repertoire of various words in various languages, and a little bit of mime to convey that I'd like to visit the church.

This nun, who is very young, seems confused and undecided about allowing me inside. Finally, I hold out a handful of lei, intending to make a contribution to the church. She backs away, and I realize she thinks I'm trying to bribe her. So I point to the money in my hand and draw a cross in the air, pointing inside the gate to convey that I mean to make a contribution to the church. She says, "Ah!", and points to my feet, I think to convey that I'm to stay where I am. She goes back inside briefly, and returns with a tiny wooden cross, hand carved, with Christ on one side and the Virgin on the other. I had noticed these same crucifixes at the other monasteries, for sale to religious pilgrims.

I smile appreciatively, and hold out the handful of lei. She carefully extracts one bill (worth a few cents) from my hand with such care it seems she believes that if she touched my skin, she's be struck dead on the spot by God. She is in the process of closing the gate in my face, when I'm saved by an older nun, and allowed in.

As I walk to the church itself, I see less activity and fewer nuns. Also, the grounds seem less well kept. There is a remote, primitive aura to the place, as though of all the monasteries of Bucovina, this is the one still living in the fifteenth century. The exterior of the church, like the others, is covered with frescoes, and seems a complete incongruity out here, surrounded by gray stone walls, and the wild hills. When I enter the church, through a covered porch where every surface of ceiling and wall is also covered with frescoes, I am soon enveloped in semidarkness. There are candles every ten feet or so on each side of a narrow nave. On the wall is a metal relief like those I've seen in the other churches. It's the Madonna and Child, the bodies made of hammered metal, the faces in ovals cut out of the metal, and painted on a flat surface. As I slowly walk down a center aisle, the flickering candlelight on the metal gives the impression the Virgin is turning to watch me.

There is a soft voice coming from a side chapel at the end of the nave. When I approach it, I find three young nuns and a fourth nun, who must be close to a hundred. They are in a circle, surrounding a small table with a candle flickering in the center. One of the young nuns is reading softly, in a monotonous drone, from the scriptures, and the others are listening. The old nun is seated, but the others stand. The sound of the young nun's voice is so even and without inflection, it is mesmerizing and I stop and stand perfectly still in the shadows, observing them. All four nuns have their heads bowed, and they are immobile. I can imagine them having been here for hours.

After a few minutes, one of the young nuns slowly raises her head and looks right at me, with a quizzical expression. It is her, I'm sure of it, in spite of the low flickering light. I can't tell if her puzzled expression comes from trying to discern if there really is someone standing here in the shadows, or if she sees me, and is trying to decide if I am who she thinks I am. Her eyes are directly on mine and even though her general expression is neutral, her eyes are becoming increasingly startled. She closes her eyes, opens them once more briefly, and collapses.

The others immediately bend over her, and one runs to the doorway of the church and calls out. Within minutes, the church is filled with nuns. The collapsed nun is lifted by four others, and carried unsteadily down the aisle. It is an eerie, funereal procession moving slowly down the nave, with candles flickering on both sides. It could as easily be 1490 as 1990.

Amazingly, no one notices me. Too much excitement in this otherwise uneventful existence. I stand motionless, long after the nuns have left the church. I am exhausted from my odyssey across Romania in pursuit of this young nun, who fainted dead-away at the sight of me, which is why I'm certain it is the same person. If I wasn't so tired (and hung over from the bad brandy the night before), I'd probably be full of fear. Fear for being here, and for making the impulsive long pilgrimage from Santorini.

It is almost dark, and while I'm still in the black corner of this mystical cathedral tucked into the foothills of the Carpathians, I hear light footsteps entering the nave. I squat down into the corner and wait. The young novice who sold me the wood crucifix, walks past with a long-handled candle snuffer in her hand having a conversation with herself, or with God, in Romanian. I can hear her reach the apse of the church and stop, and then walk a few paces and stop, and as she moves up the nave, snuffing out candles, the church gradually darkens. It is time for me to decide what to do. I could still, innocently enough, make my escape from the church, feigning absorption in the imagery if I'm encountered and challenged, and make my way out to the gate of the high stone wall. But I don't move. The young novice passes me, still talking innocently to herself and dreamily picking her nose. She stops and looks up (at God?) and then wipes her finger on the underside of a pew. She is really only a child. She continues on her way and soon the church is pitch black. I wonder if I'll be locked in, but no, she has just pulled the heavy door behind her, and I hear no locking. And why would there be? This whole compound is surrounded by twenty-foot high stone walls.

Now that I am here, alone in this cold, black, silent space, I consider the possibility of my own madness. I feel the stone, and it's smooth and cold. I reach up and touch the top of one of the fat candles, and it is indeed still warm. So, I really am here. The next question is, why? Because the compulsion to find the young nun again was so strong, I never questioned it (arguably, evidence of madness). And what I'm going to do here is enlist this intense and beautiful dark mystery person as my own Archangel Gabriel and my own Virgin Mary, and carry her off like some latter-day Filippo Lippi?

I close my eyes and when I reopen them, I don't know if I've fallen asleep, and if so, for how long. But there is a silver light lancing the darkness in several places. When I walk into the center of the nave, I see out of one of the high arched windows, an almost full moon. I walk to the door of the church, pull it open, and walk out onto the roofed porch. I lean out to see the moon, and the sky is now clear and dazzling. There is no man-made light within miles, and the sky presents itself in all its God-made brilliance, appropriately enough I think, given where I am.

In my stupor, I stand bathed in silver light, inhaling air so rich and layered and sweet, it is as intoxicating as last night's brandy. I lower my eyes to the stone buildings along the wall, the nuns' living quarters, their cells. All is dark and quiet, and just as I decide that this is the moment to make my clandestine exit, unobserved by anyone, I see in one of the small dark windows, a face lit by the moonlight, observing me as I observe her. My immediate thought is, the jig is up, and for the first time, serious panic strikes. What do Romanian authorities do to foreign men found wandering around convent grounds at three in the morning?

Then the face is gone from the window, and I think, if I run with Olympian speed to the gate, and can get it unlatched in the dark, and dash to the car, and head off into these mountains, maybe I can make my escape. The will to survive has taken over, and that's very reassuringly rationale.

But I don't run because a single figure in black is walking quickly toward me, and I conclude that since it is one nun, alone, it must be her. I am right. She says nothing, but takes my hand and leads me back inside the church. As soon as I feel her hand, I know it's the same hand that held the photographs for us to see at the villa. It is strong and callused and grips my hand as firmly as though I am some errant farm animal trying to escape her peasant grip. We go back into the church, and she leads me to a side niche, where moonlight allows us to just barely see each other.

"Why you here?", she whispers.

So many possible answers flood my numbed mind, that I am blocked and can't answer. I remain silent, just staring at her.

"Are you police?", she says this with a trace of terror, and makes a motion as though she might run for the door.

"No, I'm not the police, you know I'm from the villa on Santorini."

"Why you follow me?"

I decide to just blurt it out and fill in the details later. "I want to draw you, to paint you."

She is stunned by my answer.

Finally, a little calmer, she says, "You are artist?"

"Yes, I painted the Annunciation paintings in the small separate building by the villa." Her reaction is cautious, "I don't know what paintings you talk about."

"You saw them."

She is unnerved, and I realize that she didn't know for sure whose eyes those were peering over the base of the window from outside the chapel.

"You see me see them?" She covers her delicate mouth with her thick hand. She is silent while she remembers all I did see.

I steer the conversation elsewhere, "What is your name?"

"Sister Marina."

"That is your real name?"

"Real name is Marina Marina."

Her tone has softened and she seems resigned to having a conversation. "Why you want to paint me?"

I tell her my whole story, of having a vision of her as Gabriel and the Virgin before I even saw her at the villa, and of making the other two Annunciations.

Silence.

I ask her, "How do you know English?"

"My mother teach me."

"What does your mother do?"

"She dead."

"I'm sorry. When did she die?"

"Ten years ago."

"And your father?"

Silence

"What did your mother do that she knew English?"

"My mother was scholar of theology, brilliant scholar. That is where my name come from, I named after Saint Marina."

"Why do you call yourself, Marina Marina?" "Because there are two of me."

"Why two?, why do you say that?"

"St. Marina was daughter of pagan priest. After death of her father and then her mother, she was converted to Christian faith. Olimbrius, governor of where she live, have her arrested and he order her to renounce her

Christian religion. She refuse. She tortured and put in prison. The devil appear to her as fierce dragon and attack her. She ask God for protection, and he make dragon into dog, which St. Marina beat to death, with hammer."

"But why do you say there are two of you?"

"Because I part pagan and part Christian. I too have pagan father, a monster man, who I try to kill, with hammer, after he kill my mother, when I twelve."

"Your father killed your mother?"

"Yes."

"Why?"

"Because he tricked her, by seeming to be very different person, into being his mistress when she very young, but then she became unwilling. And he married to someone else. When I born, he pay my mother for her silence. Since he was man of most enormous power, my mother be quiet to protect me. But when I twelve, he turn his attention on me. My mother say she expose him for all he had done, and he kill her. I was there, and then I attack him with hammer, just as I know St. Marina kill the devil as dog with hammer. He recover from my attack, but is unconscious long enough for me to make my escape, to this monastery, ten years ago."

"But why didn't you go to the police, the authorities?"

"Because the police, the authorities, they answer to my father."

"But surely there were people over your father."

"There was no one in Romania over my father."

"You mean your father was...?"

"Yes, Nicolae Ceaușescu, Romania's dictator. But I never think of him as my father, to me he only my mother's murderer. So, I hide in this monastery for ten years, until last Christmas, when he is overthrown and killed, a glorious Christmas."

As Marina has told her story, we have gradually moved closer to each other, an unconscious effort to combine our bodies' heat in this frigid space. As I have listened to her, a series of scents have enveloped me: her monastery fragrances of candle smoke, incense, herbs from the garden she works in, but also the unique scent of the breath of Marina, her innocence longing for something more than her life has been till now.

"Marina, why did you think I might be the police?"

"Because my life in danger here, there are people who know of my existence, fanatical people who help overthrow Ceaușescu, people who hate him fiercely, whose hate goes to me, as his daughter, I have heard. They don't know where I am, but in time will find me.

Marina is silent again and has crouched down as though to make herself less visible as she tells her story.

She begins again, "So I hide here, and feel protected because of saints surrounding me, protected by power of pictures of saints surrounding me, do you believe pictures have power?" I laugh.

Marina is angry, "You think this joke?"

She smacks me on the mouth with her heavy callused hand, harder than I think she intended. I don't see it coming in the dark, and I'm knocked backward and stunned. I can taste blood on my mouth.

"My laugh, Marina, it was not because I think what you said is a joke, just the opposite, it was a laugh of happy surprise that you believe as much in the power of pictures as I do. It is why I am a painter, and more importantly, it is why I want to paint you as Archangel and Virgin in my final Annunciation."

"I am sorry. Pictures of saints is all I have here. Do I hurt you?"

"You drew blood."

In the first expression of any softness I've seen in her, Marina says quietly, "Oh" and she kneels down to where she has knocked me back into the corner.

Then after a moment of silence, she says, "You want to draw me?"

It is time for my monologue, and I explain more to her about my obsession with the Annunciation, and the idea of her being both Gabriel and the Virgin in the final painting, and what it means (which I really won't know until I've made the painting, although the idea is becoming more intriguing by the minute, here in this dark cold church, with this innocent young creature).

Marina is silent, and I sense skepticism, or suspicion, or something.

Finally, I say, "If you don't get out of Romania, Marina, as you say, they will eventually find you and kill you."

I don't know why this occurs to me as the final argument to make, but it works, although not for the reason I thought it would.

Marina draws her face close to mine, "You care if I killed?"

The sadness of this question, from this fugitive of ten years, is so profound that tears well up in my eyes. It is now light enough for her to see this. Dawn is breaking. She stares intently into my eyes, silently, for a full minute. She smiles, the first smile I've seen from her.

"I go to my cell, to get some things, then we leave here."

I walk with her to the door of the church. She tells me to wait for her there. I watch her short, stocky figure move through the mist rising from the grasses, and I think each of these Annunciations has its own story.

Marina is longer than I expected, and I've begun to wonder if she's changed her mind. But she finally comes through the door of the stone building that houses the nuns. She is carrying a small cloth sack, and behind her is another nun, then two, three, four, all of the small round nuns of the convent seem to have come out, single-file behind her, to see her off, like a string of black beads pulled slowly from a stone box.

They all ignore me, the whole idea of me being here at dawn is more than they can comprehend or even acknowledge. But they all know Marina's story, and they are sympathetic to whatever choice she has made to try to salvage her life.

When the heavy gate closes behind us, the sound of the metal latch causes Marina to stand briefly looking down at the ground. But then she looks at me with a small smile and proceeds to the dew-covered Dacia. When we reach the car, we both turn to look back at the monastery. The low sunlight, coming from the side, emphasizes the massiveness of the stones that have protected the church inside for five hundred years, and Marina for half her life.

***

"Martin, I'm relieved you're back. I was worried about you there, in remote Romania." "Well, I was worried about myself."

Orlando laughs and takes a sip of gin. We are once again sitting on the terrace, midst the marble antiquities bathed in late Greek light. Marina is with us on the terrace, but sitting off by herself on a stone bench silently looking out over the Aegean. I can't begin to imagine what is going on in her mind. But she seems at peace, and is fascinated by the villa and all its art, and by Orlando, who made such a fuss over her to make her feel welcome, that I think she feels adopted. In any event, the fear is gone from her eyes.

Orlando has told me, with a smile of great relief, that Hamm and Reginald are back on the island. Then he adds, with an even greater smile, "And so is Henrietta."

"Henrietta?, I'm sorry Orlando, but with all that's happened to me recently, I've lost track of the whole Arab tableau."

Orlando says, "I mean Reginald's mother, Henrietta, the blond Swedish woman who was here with the Prince, and whom we all just glimpsed momentarily."

I ask, "You mean the Prince's favorite concubine?"

Orlando winces slightly at my words, then says more soberly, "Yes, I'm afraid so."

He seems uncharacteristically flummoxed, so I move on to my burning question. "How did you get them away from that villainous character?"

Orlando smiles and says evenly, "With a Picasso. As they say, every man has his price, and the Prince's price was my early Picasso. Judging from recent appraisals, I'd say I paid seven and a half million dollars apiece for the heads of Reginald and Henrietta."

Then he adds, after tossing back rather cavalierly the last of his gin, "Sometimes Martin, it is true that money can buy everything." He looks at me with an intensity that I am to comprehend only later.

Marina asks to see the first two Annunciations again. We walk to the chapel the next morning. The interior is filled with soft light, and the paintings look strong and charged with life. Marina stands in the center of the room and looks silently at the paintings. She still wears her green-black robes, ignoring the heat. Her head is uncovered and her hair is starting to grow out, and has a softness to it, and is freshly washed and smells of Angelika's rosemary rinse. Her face is scrubbed clean and her cheeks are pink. She looks childlike and innocent, in spite of her history. She walks toward the first Annunciation.

"Okay, I touch?"

"Yes Marina, people usually don't touch paintings, but you're welcome to."

She is silent a long time, looking carefully at every surface of the work, and as she looks, she lightly runs her finger tips over the surface, over Angelika descending as Gabriel, and kneeling, and feeling the bare belly of Hanna thrust out toward her.

"She have baby?"

Marina has her hand on Angelika's hand which is over Hanna's belly, and she turns to me as she asked her question.

"Yes, Marina, she did, how did you know?"

Marina doesn't answer. She walks to the second Annunciation and kneels in front of Giulia as Virgin.

"She have baby too." Marina states this as fact.

"Yes, she did."

Marina looks at me with surprise.

"So, you think you God?" She says this sternly, as Christian, and then smiles, as pagan. With her hand still on Giulia, she says, "You love her?"

"Yes"

Marina walks to me, stands close, and takes both my hands in hers. Her hands on mine always cause a mild erotic rush, because it's the only physical contact I'm likely ever to have with her.

She watches my face carefully as she asks, "So, I Archangel and Virgin in new picture?"

"Yes."

Marina continues to watch me carefully and says, "I, in one picture say to me in other picture, we have baby Jesus inside us?"

"Well sort of, but not really."

Marina's sly pagan smile returns, "Oh, we have artist Martin's baby inside us."

Marina holds my hands tightly, as she did in Bucovina, as though I might try to literally escape her question.

"No Marina, the painting is a metaphor."

She scowls playfully, "What is metaphor?"

"It's a figure of speech, I should say, a figure of image. I'm making a picture to suggest something else, which the picture isn't."

Marina is having fun. She tips her chin down and looks doubtfully into my eyes. "You make a picture of something, but it really picture of something else." "Yes, exactly."

Now Marina is again wearing her enigmatic pagan/Christian smile.

***

Angelika embraces Marina, as does Hanna, Paolina, and even Giulia, forming a kind of new cloister for her to replace the one she left behind in Bucovina. Within a week, Marina has moved from her room in the villa and settled happily into life in Giulia's convent with the others.

Late one evening, when I'm not tired enough for bed, I'm approaching the door to Orlando's library, which is open a crack and I'm about to enter when I hear voices. One is Orlando's and the other is an unfamiliar voice, but once I hear the Swedish accent, I know that it's Henrietta's. There is such emotion in both that I'm compelled to stop and be a clandestine witness.

"Mr. Pettingill, I'm sorry." Henrietta is crying as she speaks

"Please call me Orlando."

"Yes then, Orlando, I'm sorry. I was confused, terribly confused, I owe you so much, my very life, and I do have great affection for you, but this..."

Henrietta leaves off speaking and cries softly.

I look through the narrow opening of the door. Henrietta is standing close to Orlando. She's wearing only blue panties. At her feet lies her dress. Orlando is fully dressed. He is speaking with great anguish, "But Henrietta, my love, all of our embraces, our kisses, our joyous times together celebrating your presence here, here where all I have is yours, my dear sweet Henrietta."

This is an Orlando I've never seen before and my heart aches for him.

Henrietta now begins to speak with a quaking ardor, tears streaming down her cheeks, but she is looking into Orlando's eyes.

"When you bought my freedom from the Prince, and Reginald's, I thought I will do anything for you for the rest of my life, and that's what I believed, and now that I can't be for you what you want, I feel such guilt, I feel so unworthy of your kindness. I do have feelings for you, but it's all so tied up in your saving my life."

She hesitates and breaths in several times as though gasping for air before continuing. "Hamm and I are lovers, we have been secretly for all the time he was at the Prince's palace. That is why he adopted Reginald, so that he could take him from the Prince's abuse, even if he couldn't take me."

There is a great and indescribable sound expelled from Orlando's lips, and he sinks to his knees in front of Henrietta, with his hands over his ears as though to keep out the plague.

At this, I turn and leave, overwhelmed with sympathy for both of them. Down the hallway, coming toward the library is Reginald, delivered by his usual jaunty step. I intercept him, to keep him from walking in on the scene I left behind, and ask him to take a walk with me through the olive grove.

He says, "It's pitch black out!" But to my relief he finally agrees.

***

Two months have passed. I am sitting on the floor of my studio, looking at the completed diptych: Marina as Gabriel and Marina as Virgin. The two panels are large and arched and hinged together. In the left painting, Marina in dark robes and huge black wings, spread behind her, leans forward in profile, staring intently at herself as Virgin in the adjacent panel. As Gabriel, she has a strong hand forward, fingers splayed in her gesture of authoritative pronouncement. In the right panel, Marina sits as Virgin, in white robes, her head tipped down. She is not looking to her right, at the archangel, she is looking directly out of the painting at the viewer, but more accurately, looking at me, creator of all this. She has one hand spread over her belly, and the other wrapped around the inside of her thigh.

When we first began work on the Annunciation, I positioned her so that as Virgin, she was looking across at Gabriel. But Marina kept turning her face to watch me. When I insisted she turn toward the archangel to receive the message, Marina said with stubbornness, "No, you make picture, you make message, yes? I look at you, you are Gabriel, and I am Virgin."

This was the first time someone else has said the obvious, that I am Gabriel, and Marina saying it seemed to give it authenticity. Arriving at the truth so seamlessly provoked another assertion, this time from me, "And I am also the Virgin."

I expected a whimsical smile from Marina, but she was right with me, and stared at me steadily saying, "We are each other."

Was I transcending my lifelong synthetic obstacle of: Only if she is inaccessible can I be drawn to her, but because she is inaccessible I cannot have her. I felt more intimacy with Marina than I had ever felt before, even though it was not sexual, and could not be sexual, because? Because she was like a child and because it was not meant to be. I was sure of that. It was a gift from Marina to me. As I studied her, tears streamed down my cheeks, and Marina's eyes glistened as she watched me.

Nothing more was said. The panels were then finished, over many days of intense concentration, with no mention of what transpired between us. I will love Marina forever for her childlike stubborn pursuit of the truth, a pursuit I thought I was incapable of, until she proved otherwise.

Now, when I see all three Annunciations together in the chapel, the final panel seems to say, as Marina put it, "You think you God, Martin, and art is miracle, your miracle."

I can think of nothing to say to refute that, now that I've come to understand my obsession, my obsession that is now spent, satisfied, and I am freed from.

I feel a need for some perspective on all this, perspective on a large scale. I hire a fisherman to take me across to Nea Kameni, again. In half an hour, I have walked to the edge of the volcanic crater. An enormous orange sun is balanced on the horizon. Again, I kneel and shout down into the crater.

"Now what?"

While my predecessors on Atlantis consider my question, I stand and slowly turn in a circle, surveying the sea, the surrounding islands, and Santorini. I can see the edge of the villa, and a last ray of sun strikes the blue dome of the Annunciation chapel, and as it does, I feel a thrill of liberation. The paintings are there and I am here, and as I turn slowly again, exploring each direction, the thought that runs through my mind is, I can go anywhere now, freed of my mission. As I make my decision, the sun rapidly drops out of sight, as if no longer needed to illuminate my thoughts. My decision is to leave Santorini, and take my son with me, and to return to the U.S., where I have not been for three years and where I have some unfinished family business.

In the morning, I wait by the well for the procession from the convent to collect water for the day. I wait because Giulia allows no one in the convent other than the sisters, as she calls them.

At the usual hour, they appear. Giulia says, "Hello Nicolò dear."

Little Nicolò shouts, "Daddy!", and climbs into my lap.

Angelika, Hanna, Marina, Paolina, and Sueno stand in a half-circle around me. Giulia still wears her threadbare gray Order of Poor Clares robes. Marina, her green-black Bucovinian robes. Hanna still walks around scantily clothed, to display her stigmata scars, although it's no longer an aggressive act. She seems to have recovered from her trauma and bitter response to her brother's death. She is friendly with everyone, and while she still calls her little girl Hans, she has accepted the fact that she is a girl. Hans and Nicolò have become inseparable.

They all watch me as I announce my plan.

"I'm going to be leaving, for America, and I'm taking Nicolò with me. Would you like that, Nicolò?, to come with Dad?"

Nicolò beams and nods.

There is silence while everyone considers what I've said.

Then, out from behind Hanna, comes little Hans. She is wearing a flower-embroidered white dress, with gauzy white wings pinned to the back of it, a request she made of Hanna, after seeing the Annunciation paintings. She walks to me with her swinging limp, her large blue eyes steadily on mine, her mouth open a little, suspending a thin ribbon of drool. When she's in front of me, she turns to the side and looks over her shoulder at her wings. I can see that she knows Nicolò and I are going to leave. She leans forward, her hands on her knees, her wings sticking up behind, and looks into my eyes. I have the feeling that she's urging me to look at the picture- thoughts in her mind, thoughts that are more complex than she has words for, thoughts that say, I am Nicolò's archangel, and he can't go without me.

Little Nicolò breaks the silence, "Dad, will Hans come with us to America?" There is near panic in his small voice.

I hesitate, and then say, "No, Nicolò, Hans needs to stay with her mother."

Nicolò climbs out of my lap and stands with Hans, taking her hand. He looks from one face to another around him, at the people who have given him everything he needed up to this point.

Hanna then walks over, her hard scars pink in the morning light, and squats down between Hans and Nicolò and me. She is stunning in appearance, skin golden from the Greek sun, hair long, wavy and sun-bleached a silver citron, her pale blue eyes alive and intelligent. She pulls Hans to her and then Nicolò. They press happily against her smooth warm skin. Nicolò has on faded red shorts, and combined with Hanna's extraordinary coloring, and Hans's embroidered dress and seraphic wings, they are a work of art.

Hanna turns to me and says, "Martin, may Hans and I come with you and Nicolò to America?"

The question surprises me. My reaction is the same as when Giulia said to me, five years ago, 'Can I come with you, Martin?' The difference is that now I am freed to perhaps love, and does that fact influence my answer? I don't know.

I know my life could be taking another consequential turn. I look carefully at Hanna. All that I have witnessed of her life passes through my mind: my first sight of her, emaciated, on the verge of starvation, her defiant flaunting of her belly as Virgin in the first Annunciation, pregnant by her mad twin brother, the story of being shot on the Berlin Wall, and now her apparent health and contentment as she watches me, smiling gently as though to say, 'Well, it wouldn't be so bad, would it Martin?'

I look at Nicolò, who is about to burst with anxiety, and say, "Yes, Nicolò, Hans will come with us."

Then turning to Hanna, I say, "Yes, come with us."

There is a complex choreography of movements that ends with Hanna, Hans, Nicolò, and me all crowded together, some contact between each of us, Hans pressing against me, one of her wings poking me in the chin, Nicolò straddling my knee, and the sun-warmed flesh of Hanna's hip against my arm.

A week later, the blue caique is rumbling steadily away from the villa. Standing on the wharf and waving are Orlando, Giulia, Paolina, Sueno, Marina, and Angelika. Also standing close by are Henrietta, Hamm, and Reginald, arms around each other. Orlando, in his boundless generosity has accepted them as the family they are, and has urged them to stay on at the villa for as long as they wish.

Sitting with me in the boat are Hanna, little Hans, and little Nicolò. Hanna is dressed in a skirt and T-shirt. It's the first time I've ever seen her in clothes, and it's oddly erotic. What will evolve between Hanna and me is an unknown. We are, first of all, guardians of the children, the Annunciation children, as Hanna calls them.

As we move away, I watch the blue dome of the Annunciation chapel, high on the cliff of Santorini. Then I look out over the bow of the boat. Santorini is on one side, and Nea Kameni, with its volcanic crater is on the other. In between, looking west, is the open sea, and beyond the horizon is my own Atlantis, our destination.

Part Two

The Bird Hand

The waves are large and from the south and their rhythm of arrival is regular and even. The wind, however, from the north, arrives in sporadic spurts, sending foamy whitecaps back to start again.

On my flute, my low notes are from the south. My improvised high notes are northern and facilitated by my malformed left hand, my bird hand, as my mother called it. My mother was the sculptor, Constantin Brâncuși's model (and lover, I'd always assumed until I found out differently after she was dead). My middle name is his. I am Astra Constantin Rosselli, and my hand was named by my mother after Brâncuși's Bird in Space sculptures. Not because it looks like them, my mother said, but because it will fly like them. How she knew this, I don't know, she said it when I was ten, and she's dead now twenty years.

My left hand does fly like a bird, and I can play music on my flute no one else can. I can achieve a tremolo with my bird hand that there has been no music written for, so I make up my own. I will be somewhere on this small island, as I am right now, sitting by the sea, with my dreams of the night before hidden somewhere in my mind. Some gesture of nature, it could be dramatic like the surf I observe today, or as simple as the piquant scent of tansy in the woods, will sing to my dream and waken it, and I will play my flute, improvise, and the music and the scents and the dream will all become one. When I finish playing, when the music is over, it will be gone forever.

Though the music is then lost, it's only the act of improvisation I care about. And even if I wrote it out, no one else could play this music, since no other flutist has a funny little bird hand like mine. When I say, funny little bird hand, I'm not just being a stoic, I'm being modest, because my hand is beautiful and I love it. I have always loved it, even as a child when other children teased me about it.

My bird hand starts at my wrist, because my left wrist is narrower than my right, and my whole hand is narrower, as are my fingers. I have no middle joint on these fingers (or my thumb) so there are no folds of skin there, just perfectly round, smooth, narrow fingers that turn up slightly at the tips. There aren't any fingerprints, so my left hand is like a separate person, especially since part of the inspiration for my improvisations comes from my bird hand, and part from my brain, we are a duet. When my bird fingers move over my flute, covering and uncovering so rapidly in their tremolo that all one sees is a white blur (my skin is extremely pale on that hand), it's as though a dove has alighted in a frenzy of motion and might be gone any second.

When I waken each morning, there is bright light in my eyes. My bedroom faces east, out over open ocean, and the sun is hovering just over the horizon, as though looking things over before getting down to business for the day.

The house is empty and quiet. My father has been out in his boat for an hour by now. He is a fisherman, one of a dozen on this small island that lies between Nova Scotia and Maine. My father and I moved here after my mother died. We had been living on an island in the bay of Naples. My father was struck by a terrible sorrow when my mother died, a sorrow he's never recovered from. He wanted to go somewhere completely new, hoping it would help him recover from the loss of my mother. There were distant relatives of my father's, fishermen, who came to the coast of Maine generations ago. One had been a fisherman on this island. When he drowned, my father took over his boat, and he and I have lived here since. My father is like a ghost of another time. He is kind, and we talk off and on about island matters, but in the end, it's like living alone.

This morning, as I do every morning, I watch myself in the mirror as I move about my room. I like my stride. I have long narrow legs, I am almost six feet in height. My legs are narrow but not skinny, there's a roundness to my calves and thighs, and my bottom is round as well. My ankles are strong, and my feet are a little big. I pick up my flute and continue to move around the room, playing soft tentative notes, watching myself in the mirror as I do. With my arms up, I can see the small tufts of black hair under my arms. I have never shaved any hair from my body.

I pull back my shoulders to look at my breasts which are too small, too far apart (I have wide shoulders) and too high (I have a long waist). My face is wide at my eyes, but narrows to a small chin. My mouth is small and there's a space between my front teeth. My nose is narrow, and my nostrils flare slightly. My eyes are very dark, but are blue, a kind of blue-black. They are large and seem to puzzle people when I look at them, as though I'm expressing something that I'm not. My hair is black and straight and long. I keep it pulled back away from my forehead, which is large and round (my mother told me also when I was nine, that my forehead is intelligent).

When I was twelve, I told a boy here on the island, that I had an intelligent forehead, and Italian nipples. He stared at my forehead, but it took him six months to ask if he could see my Italian nipples and I showed him. It took his twin brother six more months to ask, and I showed him too. Both became my boyfriend, and both still are. They each know the other is (my boyfriend) but have never to my knowledge discussed it (island reticence).

This morning, I dress as usual, T-shirt (faded dark green), and baggy bib overalls. I only wear shoes in winter, and since it's September, I leave my feet bare.

My breakfast is bread, which I bake twice a week, preserved fruit, and coffee that my father makes when he gets up, dense espresso. When I was ten, until I was fifteen, I drank only cafe latte, because my mother did. Then, at fifteen, I realized I was really on my own and started drinking espresso as I have for the last fifteen years. When I drink my coffee, I stand (Father says that in Italy, only tourists pay to sit at a table). I stand and look out the kitchen window at the sea and feel the caffeine race through me as I take my brief sugary sips. I have low tolerance for caffeine and within moments the fingers of my bird hand flutter, a signal to go down to the water's edge, and lure out of hiding last night's dream.

As I finish this morning's dream sonata, I think about places I've dreamed of and never been, places where my mother lived, like Estonia and Sweden, and places where my father lived, Sardinia and Sicily.

I'm sitting with my thoughts, in silence, watching the waves roll past, when I hear small giggles from above. I turn to see two small children watching me from behind the trunk of a fallen spruce. I know who they are, but this is the first I've seen of them. They are the children of a painter and his German wife, or whatever, no one knows if they're married. They have recently arrived on this island and are staying in a house on a remote point. They have kept pretty much to themselves and the islanders have not intruded. But that has not kept them from speculating about these new arrivals. By now, so many different stories have circulated, no one knows anything about them.

"Hello," I call out.

They turn to look at each other, then turn back to me again but say nothing.

One of the effects of my music, when I will it to be so, is to draw people to me. My father told me of a Capri myth of sirens who lured people to them with sweet promises implied by their irresistible music. He told me this five years ago, when there was a writer living on the island for the summer. I had read a novel of his, and it fascinated me that a man with such an interesting imagination was here so far from his cosmopolitan world. He kept to himself, and I could hear his typewriter up above as I walked along the shore.

One evening at dusk, one of those evenings when all is still and the light turns red as it diminishes, and the water is like glass, I stood still and began to play, to the light and the sweet air and the gulls circling in slow motion and holding back their cries in order to hear my music. First, I heard no more typing. Then out of the corner of my eye, I could see him standing on his porch looking down at me. Soon, he slowly wound his way down the path to the water. He asked me who I was and where I had learned to play the flute. I answered his questions and played some more. I began to walk away, along the water's edge, as I played. He followed me. Finally, I turned and said, "I'm going home, goodbye."

I played below his house three evenings in a row. Each time he was drawn from the house to the water's edge. On the third evening, he put his hand on my arm and said, "Look, can we spend some time together?"

I said, "No," and left.

Two days later, he left the island. I'd played below his house to prove I could draw him to me, and then I was satisfied. He had affected me with his writing, and I had affected him with my music. It seemed to put us on equal footing.

This morning, I blow a soft innocent song to the two children peering at me from above. They seem about four or five, and are blond and blue-eyed. The girl has one deformed leg and she dips and swings as they walk toward me. She has on a well-worn embroidered white dress, with scraggly white wings attached to the back that flop oddly as she walks. The boy holds her hand, keeping her from losing her footing as they descend the uneven slope. They sit on a rock a few feet away quietly listening to me play. As I finish, I play a run of high humorous notes and make big eyes at them. They look at each other and giggle.

"My name is Astra, what's yours?"

I look at the boy as I say this, he seems the least shy.

"Nicolò."

"And yours?" I look at the girl.

"Her name is Hans," says Nicolò.

Hans stares intensely into my eyes as though to see what my response is to her boy name.

Just as I think that it's strange that these little children are wandering by themselves above the water's edge, I look up and see a young blond woman standing in the trees above, silently watching.

"Is that your mother up above?", I ask.

"Yes and no." Nicolò says. Then, he puts out his hands, palms up, and explains. "That's Hanna up there, she is Hans's mother. Hans's father is dead. He was Hanna's brother, Hans. That's where Hans's (he nods at the girl) name comes from. My mother is Giulia, and she lives in her convent on Santorini. She thinks my father, who is Martin, is her brother Nicolò, who is dead, and that's where my name comes from. Now, do you want to hear my song?" Nicolò is pleased with his smooth delivery of the family lineage.

"Yes, I'd like to hear your song."

Nicolò climbs up on top of his rock and sings out at the waves rolling by. "Chicken in the car and the car won't go and that's the way you spell Chi-ca-go!"

Little Hans laughs so hard she falls off her rock onto the sand, knocking loose one of her wings.

Nicolò jumps down, grabs her hand, and they scramble back up the slope giggling. The blond woman above has backed out of sight.

I watch till the children have disappeared into the woods, and I pick up the small wing and go home to make my father's lunch.

***

"Hello, I've brought your daughter's wing, which she left at the beach, the tide would have taken it away."

I say this to the blond woman who had watched from the woods this morning as I talked to the children. She has just opened the door, after I stood outside and blew a few clear notes on my flute, rather than knock. This amused her and she is smiling. She speaks with a German (I assume) accent.

"Hello, we thought perhaps God was playing tricks with the wind outside the door, but then little Nicolò said..."

Little Nicolò calls out from the next room, "I said it was the lady with the funny hand." The woman shrugs and holds out her own hand to take mine. Hers is as distinctive as mine, with a hard-gnarled scar running through, front to back. "I'm Hanna, come in please."

I walk into their kitchen, always the entry to an island house.

"I'm Astra," I say, and I follow Hanna into a room with windows facing the water. There are two large tables filled with paper and drawings and drawing materials. A man is bending over, drawing, and he straightens. He is in his early forties, blond and blue-eyed, medium height (shorter than I), even featured, and seems preoccupied with his work.

He says, "Hello, I'm Martin."

He comes over and takes my hand, my normal hand, I only offer my bird hand when I want to have an effect on someone. But then some impulse I don't understand, tells me to switch hands and I do. Martin briefly feels my hand carefully and then smiles at me.

The children are side by side on the floor, drawing. Little Hans is on her stomach and still in her white dress with its one wing protruding crookedly. She sees her other wing in my hand and comes over to claim it. After she takes the wing from me, she stares steadily into my eyes. She seems to be looking to see where I found it. I realize now that Hans either cannot or will not speak.

"It was by the water's edge, Hans, the ocean was about to take it home with her."

Hans smiles and reaches for my hand to take me over to her drawing. When she sees that she's taken my normal hand, she drops it and reaches for my bird hand. She takes it in both hands and studies it as she leads me to where she and Nicolò were drawing. We both kneel down to look at her picture, which is of herself lying on her stomach drawing, with one wing sticking up. She picks up a blue crayon and with her tongue protruding from the corner of her mouth and a string of drool suspended from it, she carefully draws in her other wing.

Nicolò is drawing by her side, idly singing. "Wing off the angel and the angel won't go and that's the way you spell Chi-ca-go."

When Hans finishes her drawing, she stands and hands it to me, a gift.

Hanna and Martin tell me their story. They have come to the island from Chicago, Martin's home, but before that they were on the island of Santorini in Greece.

Martin says, "We came to this island because I wanted to be far from Chicago, where tragedy struck my family. Six months ago, my parents were killed in a car accident. I'd had a falling out with them years ago and I returned to Chicago from Santorini to try to make peace with them. They were difficult and silent people, and even though we were beginning to try and understand each other, they died before any reconciliation could take place. I told Hanna when we left Chicago that I wanted to go somewhere remote where I could deal with my sorrow. When we came here to the coast of Maine looking for a place, we were told by a rental agent about a woman whose husband had died on this island and who wanted to rent out her house and leave, which is of course this house."

As I listen to Martin, I'm struck by the similarity of his story and my father's, each had lost close family in death, each had wanted a remote place to grieve in peace, and each had ended up here because of another's tragedy: my father's fisherman relative who drowned, and the husband of the woman in whose house Martin and Hanna and the children now lived, who had died here.

When I point this out, in all its symmetry, and use the words coincidence and accident, Martin says, "You know, I've come to believe there are no accidents, no coincidences, there are only reasons why things happen, and only later do we understand the reasons."

Martin says this with such feeling, that everyone in the room pauses in silence, even the children, to consider why we might all be here under the same roof.

Finally, Nicolò says, "Dad, here's a new one: Why Astra's in our house we don't know and that's the way you spell Chi-ca-go."

He and Hans get up, and holding hands, twirl around us while Nicolò sings out repeatedly, "Why Astra's in our house, we don't know, why Astra's in our house, we don't know, why Astra's in our house, we don't know," until he and Hans end up giggling uncontrollably. And while the children continue to twirl around us laughing, Martin and Hanna and I look at each other while we consider the same question.

Finally, Martin says, "Anyway, we started out from Santorini, that's where Nicolò's mother, Giulia, is."

I am about to say, in the convent? But I decide not to reveal that Nicolò has already reported on the story of their lives. Anyway, Nicolò may have made it up.

But then, Hanna says that Hans's father, also named Hans, is on Santorini too, in spirit. She doesn't say he was her brother. She is silent and looks out the window after she has spoken.

After a moment of silence, Martin says, "Astra, I'm embarrassed to tell you this, but you've had an audience each morning since we've been here, as you played your flute down by the shore. I hope you don't mind. We didn't want to disturb your playing so we stayed out of sight up above, listening, until this morning when the children decided to make your acquaintance."

Hanna turns to me, "Your playing is so beautiful, Astra, and so sad all at once, such sweet melancholy, but at the same time, such angst, but perhaps that is just in me. It is all improvised, isn't it? I mean it comes and goes, the music, never to be repeated, like moments in life. Where does it come from, this music?"

"Well, usually it starts with a dream the night before, and whatever is happening as I play, I mean, what the sea and sky are doing, and how it all affects my mind."

Hanna says, "Music of dreams, that's what I said to Martin."

As I watch Hanna, I see that her other hand also has a scar. She sees that I see this, and she pushes off her sneakers, and I see that her feet too have hard red scars. She watches me watch her hands and feet, and she pulls up her T-shirt to just below her breast and reveals another scar, on her right side. She straightens her body and puts her arms out to the side, crosses her feet, and tips her head down so that her long curls cover her shoulders.

"Crucifixion, Astra, no?"

I'm caught by surprise by this display and say, "No, yes." Hanna smiles then, and relaxes back in her chair.

Nicolò is singing to himself as he draws, "Scars on the feet and the feet won't go and that's the way you spell Chi-ca-go."

Hanna says matter-of-factly, "Bullet wounds from climbing the Berlin Wall, escaping from the east. My brother Hans had the same scars. He killed himself, on Santorini."

So, Nicolò's story so far is true.

After a few moments, Martin says, "Astra, about your music, have you thought about taping your improvisations so that they're not lost forever?"

I reply, "I only play at certain times, when I want to play, for myself. I couldn't go into a recording studio and play, just like that, it wouldn't mean anything, and it wouldn't be very good. I play in response to my dreams, to my experiences, it's very spontaneous, very unplanned. In order to record my music, I'd have to be living somewhere as beautiful and inspiring as this island, and I'd have to live surrounded by recording equipment that I could just flip on with a switch and either play or not, it would all have to be no more intrusive than that."

Martin and Hanna look at each other as though each has had the same thought.

***

A week goes by, and though I've had fleeting glimpses of Nicolò and Hans in the woods up above, like little wood sprites, I am alone as I play each day down by the water.

Then one morning Hanna and Martin appear and sit off at a distance until I'm through playing. They come over, and Hanna takes my hand and says, "So strangely beautiful, Astra."

Martin says, "Astra, what do you think of this idea? On Santorini, where we have lived, there is a villa and a man who owns it, where, how shall we say, art occurs and is preserved. Last night, I talked on the phone with this man, whose name is Orlando Pettingill, a wealthy art collector and aesthete, a man whose whole life is dedicated to art, of all kinds, including music. I told Orlando about your music, and Hanna also talked to him. We told him that every time you played, the music was then lost for-

ever. I reminded him that he once had a group of Bolivian musicians staying at the villa, and that he had installed recording equipment for them in
one of the terraced rooms overlooking the Aegean Sea. They could play,
and record or not, when they wanted, just by flipping a switch, as you say.

"Orlando said, 'She's welcome, and all the equipment is still here. I'll
cover her expenses, getting here and all. If she's as promising as you say,
we certainly should do it."

I'm stunned by all Martin has said and feel suddenly invaded, and
without thinking, I say, "I never said I was promising, and I never invited
anyone to hear me play." After I say this, I realize how aggressive it sounds,
as though I resent their having listened to me play.

Hanna comes to me and puts her hand on my cheek. She stares into
my eyes. Her own clear blue eyes seem imbued with a sorrow too large for
her age, but there is also anger in her voice as she says, "I'm sorry, Astra,
we won't come to hear you play again."

Her hand feels wonderful on my cheek, which she is stroking. I can
feel her sad scar moving against my skin. A wave of warmth moves from
my cheek to my neck and to my shoulders, turning my skin blush-red, I'm
sure. Her sadness, her life sadness it seems, is so moving.

Hanna's expression as she watches me is puzzling. It seems a plea of
sorts.

She says, "Hans, my brother, let his art too, slip away forever, only he
was tied to it as it plunged into the sea."

I have no idea what Hanna means about her brother, and I'm afraid to
ask. None of us seems to have more to say. Finally, as I move to sit on a
rock, I take Hanna's hand to pull her down alongside me. We sit in silence

and look out at the water, which is not wavy, or calm, but sort of in-be-tween, irregular choppiness, like a reflection of my thoughts, agitated and inconsistent.

Finally, I stand, face Hanna, and begin to play tentative notes on my flute, notes that search for some comprehension of how I feel. A form be-gins to evolve, and soon I'm playing a passage laced with high, darting, sliding sounds. Hanna is motionless and stares fixedly at me as I play.

Then I turn to Martin, and a new passage emerges, slower and lower sounds, more steadily rhythmic, as though he's the reassuring element in all this. As Martin listens, he smiles slightly in a way that relieves me. He also stares at me with an intensity that seems a curiosity on his part of just who I really am, in a deep private sense, almost intimate sense.

Then I begin to combine the paean to Hanna and the paean to Martin and as I do, he moves to sit beside Hanna, where I was sitting.

Then a third, middle range of notes and tempo slides up and down the scale to loop everyone together. This element is me, I realize after I'm play-ing it, combining my life with Hanna's and Martin's with an assurance that seems arrogant. When I finish, we three listen to the final notes diminish to silence as they are carried with the light breeze up into the woods. Little Nicolò and Hans come down the slope as though called forth by my notes. They climb together into the laps of Martin and Hanna, and all four silently watch me. I turn to look at the sea. It's as calm as I now feel, and for the first time, I regret that one of my pieces is again gone forever.

The following morning, I wake to a dark day and a driving rain. This will be an interior day, both in the sense that I'll stay inside to play my flute, and that my thoughts will be turned inside, to memory. My first thought is yesterday's encounter on the beach with Martin and Hanna. My flute is on the table by my bed, and I take it and stand in front of the mirror to play.

As I look at myself, I imagine hard red scars on my own hands and feet, and in my side. What a remote life I lead on this island, while Hanna and Martin, and even the children, have seen so much. For the first time, I think of leaving the island, and that surprises me.

I've never questioned life here before. It's been so reassuringly predictable. Even being at college on the mainland didn't alter my feelings about the island. At school, everyone either seemed preoccupied with trivia (the students) or academic detachment (the faculty). Only the few foreign exchange students fascinated me. But they all went back home again.

I made do with the attention of the twins here on the island (they are really interchangeable), even though my mind often wanders in my encounters with them, like recently when I was standing in the woods, holding my flute and looking out at the water. One of my twin boyfriends was standing behind me. I was remembering a dream of the night before.

I was in a remote village along the Amazon and surrounded by native men. They were dark, with bright painted markings on their bodies. It was some sort of religious ceremony, and they were forbidden to touch me, but all stared boldly at my body. As I stood with the twin behind me, he started to unbutton the straps of my overalls at the front. I let him do this and my overalls dropped to my ankles. As I blew into my flute, the dream scene was vivid, and I was staring at a stiff aboriginal phallus, pointed and covered with brightly painted markings.

The twin was fumbling behind me with one of his candy-colored condoms, while I was playing probing notes on my flute. With my eyes closed, impaled and surrounded by small savages shaking bright hued erections up and down in their stiff primordial dance, I played high rain forest bird songs on my flute. My climax, musical and otherwise, was a series of shrill, trembling tremolos that had the black ravens in the woods, and the white gulls over the water, shrieking back at me.

As I walked home, I thought to myself, I love my flute, my music, my dreams, but except for my mother and father, I've never loved another person. And I wondered if I ever would, wondered if I was capable of it.

"Orlando's villa is enormous and filled with paintings and sculpture, from classical Greek to Brâncuși."

Martin is describing Santorini. We are sitting on the floor of the living room of Hanna's and Martins house. It is late and the children are in bed. We're surrounded by the last of our late supper, sipping wine and eating cheese and grapes. The rose and feta are both from Santorini, and have prompted discussion about life on that island, many thousands of miles away.

I'm caught by surprise at the mention of Brâncuși. After a moment, I ask, "If I go to Santorini, will Orlando let me touch his Brâncușis?"

Martin is amused. "Yes, Astra, I'm sure he wouldn't mind, but why?"

"Because my mother was a model for Brâncuși, in the early fifties, near the end of his life, in Paris. She died when I was ten, but much later I found a journal of hers and in it she wrote about Brâncuși. She was eighteen when she met him, and a model for a painter in Paris, and Brâncuși visited the painter's studio one day when he was drawing my mother, nude. He immediately asked her to model for him. She thought he wanted sex, because he was so adamant. My mother didn't consider herself beautiful, in fact she had a body like mine, too lanky, but round in places. As is turned out, it was that long body of my mother's that Brâncuși wanted to work from for some of his sculptures, some tall stone pieces that combined curves with crisp angles.

"She described Brâncuși as tall, and always dressed in white. His hair and beard were long and also white. There was marble dust everywhere and the whole experience she said seemed ghostly and dreamlike. She was wrong about his wanting sex with her, his interest was in transcendence. But he wanted to look at and feel her body, and absorb those sensations into his sculpture. In between carving on the stone, he would walk to her and move his hands over her body. His hands were large and rough. If he was working on a curvilinear portion of the sculpture, he would feel her calves and thighs, her bottom, her belly. For the angular portions, he would feel her chin line, her clavicle, her shoulders, the crisp shelf of her hip bones, her shins and ankles. He was totally silent as he worked. He never talked to my mother and he never made the slightest sexual advance. His art was his life as well as his libido. That's why I want to be able to feel the first Brâncuși sculpture I see."

Later, after looking at some drawings of Martin's and some sketches for a performance piece that Hanna was working on, we go to bed. I'd told my father I wouldn't be home that night, and he nodded, seeming unconcerned about his being alone. On Hanna's and Martin's couch, I felt enriched by the presence of all of them elsewhere in the house, and my father's nonchalance about me being elsewhere had a disarming effect on my usual sense of belonging in my house on the island, and the feeling of attachment that always comes with it.

In the morning, after breakfast, Hanna and the children leave to walk to the island store, and I am about to walk home in the opposite direction. Instead, I stop by the water below and begin blowing soft notes on my flute. I'm thinking of how when I'm with Martin, he studies me so carefully. There is an energy in the air that seems related to the fact that we both use words sparingly, and never in our work. His staring seems both to ask, 'who are you?', and to declare, 'I need to know you.' He makes no effort to conceal his interest, but at the same time he seems uneasy with his interest. I begin to play a luring improvisation and before I'm finished, Martin is standing by my side.

"You know, Astra, the power of art has been the puzzle of my life. I felt physically drawn down here by your playing just now. Was that your intention? Like the sirens of Capri?" He only half smiles as he says this.

I consider acting innocent, but instead I say, "It is what I wanted. I've never known people like you and Hanna before. You are affecting my life so much and so quickly. You are lucky to have each other."

"Hanna and I don't have each other. We are together for the sake of Nicolò and Hans.

Hanna has terrible demons that prevent her from, well, connecting, I guess is the right word."

"Then you are not...?"

"Lovers? No, and we have never been."

"Is that why you feel free to stare at me?"

Martin is surprised at my directness, as am I.

"Astra, there's something about your music that pulls the truth out of me, or more accurately, would pull the truth out of me, if I let it. I stare at you because I have my own demons."

"That is all very vague, but very scary. I'm a provincial islander, you know."

"You may be a provincial islander, Astra, but you're an artist of immense power, and, you're also..."

Martin doesn't finish, so I say, "I'm also what?"

Martin shakes his head slightly as though to dismiss the question, looks out to sea for a moment and says, "My obsession with the power of

art, you'll see on Santorini in the form of three paintings, three Annunciation paintings. And on Santorini, you'll find the players in the three paintings, amazing women still there at the villa, all of them artists in direct and
indirect ways. Hanna is the only one not there. You'll meet them all, and
they'll affect your life as they have mine."

As though picturing them in his mind's eye, Martin pours forth their
stories, as we walk along the water's edge. It takes a long time and when
he finishes, he pauses again to silently watch the ocean.

"Martin, what were you going to say before when you said I was
also..." He turns to me, looking at my face with his painter's assessing eyes.
"Uniquely and intriguingly beautiful, inside and out."

I'm caught by surprise and I blush.

"I'm sorry Astra, I didn't mean to embarrass you."

As he says this, he places his painting hand softly on my cheek, surprising me further. I look at him carefully before surprising myself by putting my bird hand on his cheek, producing a slight tremor. Nothing more
is said, and the only sound is the rolling ocean caressing the boulders below, the ocean that thousands of miles east merges with the sea that slaps
at the edge of Santorini. The following morning, while playing a soft paean
to celebrate the presence in my life of Martin and Hanna and the children,
but especially Martin, I decide to accept Orlando Pettingill's invitation to
visit Santorini and tape my music, to meet him and all the players of the
villa, as Martin calls them, the players whose lives I already know so much
about from Martin, and who have affected him so deeply. Why do I feel
such urgency to be where he was, and with whom he used to be, to sub-
merge myself in what has so affected him as an artist, and a man? He is
affecting me too much, and some of the music I play when he's on my mind

is, well, lyrically lascivious. Now, there's a new musical term. At this admission, I know it's time to leave here. And I can't begin to figure out my feelings toward Hanna, beyond my guilt at, it seems, coveting Martin, even if she doesn't.

It is in this state of agitation that during our usually silent dinner, that evening, I tell my father that I'm leaving the island.

I make my announcement as he's taking a sip of wine, which misses his mouth, running down his chin. He wipes the wine away and stares at me with an intensity that I've not seen since my mother died. I quickly proceed to give him all the information that led to my decision, emphasizing the opportunity to have my music taped, trying to make it seem less personal.

He looks out the kitchen window at the dusk dotted with circling gulls, studying them as though at some moment they will form a constellation in the sky that will be a clue, a clue to how he is feeling, a clue to what he wishes to say. Just when I'm beginning to think that he's not going to say anything at all, he softly embarks on the longest soliloquy I've ever heard from him.

"Maybe you think I not have you in my mind here, that I am alone here. What is true is total different from that. Since you went from child to Astra the woman, when you become say, nineteen years, your mother she come back to this house, to me, because you so like her, how you look, how you talk, how you walk, how you eat, even how you smell. Maybe you think this terrible that your father smell you, but that the way it is. There you are, both my daughter and my wife and it make me frightened. In my boat, by myself, on the sea where all can be anything, then I talk to you, out loud, but it is to you as your mother, but still you, and because sometimes, the difference is like fog, hard to see through, then I worry maybe I have a mind that is going out to sea, with the tide, till one day my mind is gone. In the meantime, I afraid to say something wrong to you, or do something wrong, in this mixing of two people so equal important to me that they become one."

Then my father sits still and stares at his huge callused hands that are moving over each other as though to feel if the right words have been said.

After a moment I say, "Everything you said, Papa, I understand and I'm proud that you think of me sometimes as my mother, I take it as a wonderful compliment, a gift really.

At this, he looks up into my eyes and every crease the ocean has made in his face collaborates in the largest smile he's ever given me.

He says, "It OK that I think like this?"

I say, "It's better than OK, it's beautiful."

We both stand and he envelopes me in his wiry arms, and holds me against him with the certainty that I am indeed his daughter and that only by telling me his story was he able to disentangle the ghost of his wife from the life of his daughter.

Finally, he says, "Grazie, Astra, and you will go to Santorini and take with you the blessing of your mother and your father."

***

The sea swells are deep and rhythmic and everyone on board is sick, except me. Even the Greek men have ceased their comic attempts at seduction and are down below, groaning and cursing as manfully as they can. I am crying quietly with joy at being again surrounded by sea and islands. The Aegean is a greener blue than the Atlantic I'm used to, and these islands are as bald as mine are richly forested, but the sense of expanse and endless possibilities is the same and, in my way, I feel again at home.

By the time we reach Santorini, the sea has gone from even swells to swollen turbulence. It is too rough to dock the huge ferry, so a small launch comes out from the harbor to meet us. A large side hatch is opened in the hull of our ship that is about level with the launch. Unbelievably, the dozen or so passengers begin to board the launch with a combination long step and leap timed as carefully as possible so that the two vessels are at about the same level. Greek deck hands are shouting over the slapping splash of water and propelling the passengers across the foamy chasm. My own leap seems a prelude to my odyssey from what is known to the unplayed music that lies ahead. Our baggage is thrown across after us, the lines are loosened, and we're on our way to the port of Thera.

Following Martin's instructions, I've asked for a certain fisherman and he takes me in his caique to the wharf of Orlando Pettingill's villa. This fisherman is as reticent as my father and I think again of our last conversation and I have a rush of homesickness, and loneliness, here in this exotic place where I know no one.

Standing alone on the wharf as the caique rumbles back toward the port, I survey my surroundings. Across the water is the dormant volcanic island of Nea Kameni, where, Martin told me, lies the lost city of Atlantis. I stare in awe and decide that the only possible response to it all is music. I take my flute from my pack and leaning in the shade against a rock wall next to a cluster of vertical cables, close my eyes, take a deep breath and project out across the water my first response to this new world. As always, I embrace in my playing the sounds around me. There is the irregular slap of water against the stone wharf, a wind whistling into the crevices of the cliff above, and finally a low moaning sound that I don't attempt to identify, I accept it as a partner in a counterpoint. It slowly gets louder and then stops, and when it does, my improvisation also ends. I stand with my eyes closed until all traces of my music have wafted out to sea.

When I open my eyes, a few feet away is an ornate metal elevator cage whose descent I now realize provided the mechanical moan I played against. Out of the elevator steps a short, square dark woman, dressed in green-black robes. She seems to be staring at me but she isn't. She is blind, and Martin has told me her story, how she suddenly lost her sight on Santorini, after Martin had left. She has a strong but sadly resigned face, and is moving toward me with a hand out front.

"Hello, I am Marina, ah!"

She places a hand on the side of my face and begins to carefully examine my features. We are both silent as Marina satisfies her curiosity about my appearance. She puts her other hand on my head, feeling my hair, and then moves both hands down to my neck and shoulders. She has had to reach up considerably to do all of this, and finally says, with an accent, "You are very high."

Her hands are large, strong, and rough. I was told that she's been making stone sculptures since her blindness. She runs her fingers down my arms to take my hands. When she feels my bird hand, she moves her other hand over to it too, and while she thoroughly examines it she says, "We told about this magic hand in letter from Martin, it so fine and smooth, OK that I touch it?"

"Yes, of course."

Marina still has hold of my hand, and leads me to the elevator. We go up several hundred feet, and out beyond the cliff is the Aegean and its islands, and I'm fascinated because I've never had this bird's eye view of ocean at home. Waiting on a platform at the top of the cliff is Orlando Pettingill, whom Hanna described as a great frog prince, and she's right. Froglike because of his large protruding eyes, and great jowls that inflate and deflate as he breaths and speaks. Prince-like, because he is so gracious.

"Astra, I'm so pleased you've come, so honored, welcome, I'm Orlando."

As we walk up to the villa, he asks about Martin and Hanna, both of whom he speaks of with great fondness.

Martin had told me the villa was filled with art, but I didn't expect it to be so like a museum, in the amount and quality of art, all interwoven with the function of life in the villa. I have never experienced such wealth. The villa is huge, room after room, on several levels, cool marble floors, vases of flowers everywhere, everything immaculate, clean smelling, the fragrance of wealth, I decide. But the fact that all this money is dedicated to art, redeems it. I have inherited my mother's Estonian, and my father's Neapolitan suspicion of wealth, but here in this villa somehow I feel that I and my music and all the art and affluence around me are on equal footing.

I am shown to a room by Hamm, the tall formal man who oversees the villa. With him is his adolescent son, Reginald, who is carrying my pack, and not very subtly surveying my body. I'm wearing high-cut hiking shorts and a T-shirt. Martin has told me about them, and also Henrietta, Reginald's mother and now Hamm's wife, the whole story a bizarre tale worthy of the Brothers Grimm.

My room is simple, elegant, and filled with art, with doors opening onto a terrace that overlooks the sea and the islands.

Hamm says, "We suggest this room until you've had an opportunity to look over the villa and decide where you'd like to stay, and to play your music." He adds, "Mr. Pettingill invites you to join him and some others this evening for drinks on the antiques terrace, before dinner."

"A gin on the antiques terrace, you know, Martin said that was the closest to heaven he'd ever get."

"Ah yes, we all miss Martin, and Hanna, and the children."

Hamm's smile has a trace of sadness to it, and I realize how much he's probably witnessed here at the villa in the name of art. He turns to leave, as does Reginald, after one last comical ogle.

I sit on a stone bench on the terrace with my arms on the long marble balustrade that is graced in one corner with an antique marble female figure who has no nose or arms. I move my nose down against my arm and as I breath in the sweet scent of the sun on my skin, I sympathize with this smooth white figure who cannot do the same. But then, she has no skin fragrance to smell, although she must have some fragrance, some scent of a couple of thousand years of exposing her creamy white body to the world, and for a while she did have a nose to enjoy it. I'm very tired from my travels, and when I'm tired I occupy myself with small immediate matters, what's close by, and she's just a few steps away. I walk over to her corner of the terrace. She is slightly smaller than life-size and facing out to sea. Her face is turned to the right. With one foot up on the balustrade and stretching, I can look into her eyes. Her face is plain and wind-worn, timeless and resigned. She has seen a lot. The pupils of her eyes are deep indentations and their shadows give her a lifelike gaze.

"Is it OK that I do this?" I ask her quietly as I lightly touch her cheek with my nostrils. The marble is warm from the sun and smooth and the aroma archly distinct. I cannot in my mind find anything to compare it to. I finally decide it's the scent of history, her history. I move my nose over her forehead, down across her eyes, her lips, under her chin where because of the shadow, the redolence changes slightly, is moist, musky, motherly. That seems a clue to something, so I find a deep shadowy place where her hair forms a curve over her shoulder. Where the marble is darkest and shadowed and green, I inhale deeply and again it's the redolence of history. It's not a human fragrance, but it's a fragrance of human history, and I can only think of my mother, my Estonian mother, my mother as a Brâncuși sculpture, and a play of words softens my sadness... my stony Estonian mother. I say the words softly aloud, and smiling I turn to go fetch my flute. In the doorway, someone is standing perfectly still, watching me.

"I knock, I hear no answer," she says matter-of-factly.

I know who she is because of Martin's careful description of her. It is Angelika. I recognize her from her dark Greekness, her black clothes, the three moles in a row on her cheek, and her slight mustache. I don't know how long she's been watching me and I'm embarrassed and I feel spied upon.

She is holding a tray.

"I bring tea, you like it out here?"

"Yes, thank you, on the bench would be fine."

She puts the tray down and smiling conspiratorially says, "I smell all statues in villa, when no one watching, long ago smells make me know people who have come and gone long time ago, makes my nose history book."

"Yes, that's true, hello Angelika, I'm Astra."

"Hello, I know who you, how you know me?"

"Martin described you."

"Aha, Martin. He tell you about my three islands in olive sea that drown when I smile?"

I laugh and say, "Sit down and have tea with me."

"Only one cup."

"We'll share it."

Angelika drowns her islands and sits down close to me on the stone bench and we pass the cup back and forth, stopping to refill it twice from the pot.

"Martin and Hanna both said to say hello."

Angelika looks out across the water toward the west, toward America. After a moment she says, "I love Martin, I love Hanna." She shrugs her shoulders slightly and says nothing more. After a minute of silence, she picks up the tray and walks from the terrace. At the doorway, she turns, smiles, and wiggles the fingers of one hand in a funny little wave and leaves.

"Ah Astra, good evening."

This is Orlando, and his ebullience seems aglow from the late Aegean sun that wraps the terrace and the many marble sculptures in a pinkish patina.

This terrace too is surrounded by a marble balustrade with sculptures in each corner, in addition to others on the open marble floor, all Greek and Roman. There are a dozen or so people on the terrace, in several small groups talking and drinking. I mostly listen. Later, dinner is a rather grand event. Orlando likes to eat, and there are a number of courses, all superb and served by Angelika who grins at me several times as she moves around the table. The conversation moves from subject to subject. No one asks me what I do or why I am here, and I'm thankful for that. I wonder though if they've been cautioned by Orlando. When dinner is over, close to midnight, I can hardly keep my eyes open, and I say goodnight.

Standing naked in the dark of my terrace, I can see vague shapes of islands out to sea, the dark silhouette of the Vulcan across the bay, and a cruise ship anchored below, lights ablaze, like a tiny bathtub toy. The sky is clear and embellished with unfamiliar constellations. It is perfectly quiet. The air is warm and laced with scents of citrus and rosemary and sunbaked stone and clay. I feel as though I could be anyone, at any time, and I move my hands over my body to attest that I am indeed me standing here on the verge of my new universe.

My knowledge of the villa's inhabitants that I have from Martin, gives me an odd feeling of connection to them, but they know nothing of me. So, the music I play at first is to draw them to me, to interest them in me, to know something of me, to even the score.

This morning, I'm sitting in a patch of shade within sight of the pristine white stone building they call the convent, that sits on a knoll some distance back from the villa, and my music this morning is a plea for friendship. I start with low soft probing notes which are more an expression of how I feel, than a call to others. I look up to the sky and I see white gulls circling slowly high overhead. The breeze has picked up and I'm moved to send notes soaring on that wind to circle above the convent, to pierce the self-sufficiency of these players in Martin's life and paintings.

Soon, from around the corner of the building come three women, two dressed in brightly patterned Gypsy clothes. I recognize them from Martin's description. One is Paolina, sister of Giulia, little Nicolò's mother, who now also emerges from behind, and the third is Paolina's girlfriend, the Gypsy, Sueno. They are all looking up at the sky to find my music which has now drifted off. I sit silently and watch as they talk among themselves and look around, puzzled. As they turn to go back inside, I blow three separate warbling notes, one for each of them. They are sweet, beautiful calls. One by one, each as she hears her own note, turns to observe me. I animate the notes and combine them to make a small luring song, and smiling, they walk toward me.

The Gypsy Sueno, has nothing to say, but she is smiling from the music. Her coloring is so exotic, I could play to her all day. Everything is visually contradictory; her eyes and hair are lighter than her skin, and her teeth gleam like white marble. Her eyes are a light soft brown mixed with a pale gray, and the word that comes to mind is ghostly, I think because her beauty is frightening.

Giulia is also quiet as she approaches. I'm uneasy with how much I know about her, that she was Martin's love, and now lives in an inner world that is not sane. She's dressed in old nun's robes, worn and patched soft gray. She too is smiling, vacantly, apparently also from my music.

Paolina, however, more than makes up for the reticence of the others. "So, you're Astra. Hello, I'm Paolina." She eyes my bird hand as she says this, so I give her that hand in greeting.

"Ohhhh," she says as she studies it with her startling blue eyes. "This hand is so magical, so fine and delicate and smooth, so unique. My left hand is the same as my right, same with my feet, symmetry is so boring.

Sueno watches me with her pale apparition eyes to see what my response is to this contingent from the convent.

Paolina turns to Giulia and back to me saying, "This is my sister, Giulia, but I guess you know who she is. Giulia, this is Astra, she's come from the island in America where little Nicolò is."

Giulia laughs and says, "Little Nicolò? He's no littler than I am."

Martin has told me about her confusion, so I just smile and say, "Hello Giulia," and hold out my bird hand.

Giulia looks at my hand with a frown, and occupying both her hands arranging the collar of her robes, says, "Hello Astra," and smiles vacantly.

Paolina, in another burst of energy, says, "Astra, come into the convent and we'll have tea. At this, Giulia shows slight panic.

Paolina says, "Oh, okay, Giulia. Then, turning to me, she says, I have to go over to the villa, Astra, will you walk with me?"

I say yes, and Giulia and Sueno turn back towards the convent.

As Paolina and I walk together, she punctuates her words with gentle Italian hand gestures and I think of my father and how his hands always seemed to be apologizing for his words.

"You have to forgive Giulia, she's a little crazy. The reason she objected to your coming into the convent is that any break in routine upsets her. Once she knows in advance that you're coming, she'll be okay. Also, the reason she wouldn't take your hand is that anything anatomical that's not normal scares her. She's had bad experiences with wounds because of her brother, but that's a long story. Not that your hand is a wound, I know it's always been like that, but to Giulia it's just not right. Hanna's scars really upset her, so she wouldn't look at them, which meant she had to practically pretend Hanna didn't exist since Hanna walked around naked most of the time just so everyone would see her scars.

"But I love your hand." At this Paolina pulls my bird hand up and rubs it softly against her cheek.

"So Astra, do you want to come visit the convent? you could come on bath night, visit our Romanian bath, as Marina calls it. It's very soothing, very calming. We heat up water in the sun all day, then fill the cistern in the convent, we throw in lots of lavender and rosemary and citrus rinds, light candles, and we bathe each other. You'll like it, we do it on Saturday night. I'll tell Giulia you're coming and she'll be fine, Okay? Saturday? Come around nine."

Paolina runs ahead, waves, and disappears into the kitchen of the villa.

Back on the balcony of my room, I stand facing the sea and play a sonata to the three women I've just been with. Playing is gratifying because it
gives a form to each of them. But I also feel an anxiety that so much is happening so quickly. So many new people in my life and each so different.
Suddenly I'm crying, feeling a sense of loss. I am grieving over the loss of
the music I've just played, and have been playing since I've been here at the
villa, and I realize it's time to start taping my music. How will this affect
my life, is a thought that frightens me, am I going to become a performer?,
For whom? And what does that mean?

***

It is the night of my Romanian bath. Standing a little below the convent, I bring my flute to my lips. I remember the note I've assigned to Paolina, and I deliver it again with warble and whimsy to bring her forth.
Within seconds she appears from around the corner of the white washed
stone building, now pinkish in the late Greek light. Paolina jumps up once
and claps her hands before running down the slope to greet me. She is nude
and her small body is impish and perfect. "Hi Astra, you're here just at the
right time, come in, we're bringing in water from the terrace."

She grins and looks quickly to make sure it's my bird hand she's taken
as she leads me up the slope. We enter a narrow door at one end of the
convent. It's almost dark inside, even with some candles burning steadily
in the still evening air. At the opposite end of the building, a large open
doorway with stone columns on either side allows the evening light to enter, delineating the circular stone cistern in the center of the floor. In and
out of this doorway move the other women of the convent, naked caryatids
shouldering earthenware amphorae of water that's been heating up all day
on the sunny terrace.

Each empties her vessel with a festive splash and returns for more. I feel self-conscious in my clothes, and begin to peel them off. Paolina helps, anxious to have me part of the ritual. Everyone smiles and greets me, especially Giulia who says, "Oh Astra, I was afraid you wouldn't come."

I help with the water, and as I do, I observe the others in the diminishing light, and they observe me. Among us we are a rich repertoire of female presence:

Our height ranging from my just under six feet, to Marina's, a full foot shorter, with Paolina and Angelika closer to Marina, and Giulia and Sueno in the middle.

Our eyes, from Giulia's pale ethereal blue, to Sueno's pale mystery gray, to the progressively deeper blue of Paolina and me, to the irises of Angelika and Marina, so dark they merge with the pupils they encircle.

Our bodies, from Paolina's small perfection, to my long imperfection, to Angelika's sleek darkness, to Marina's modesty, to Sueno's dusty-flesh firmness, to Giulia's pale rosy roundness.

Our hair, there's more dark than light, with Marina, Angelika, Paolina, and me equally black, Sueno a little lighter with some umber, and finally dear Giulia's pale yellow so light it seems she's trying to merge with the Santorini sunlight to complete her removal from this reality.

As I observe these women, I'm self-conscious at all I know of them from Martin. My uneasiness soon dissolves with the lovely warm water that is being carefully poured over me from several directions. It was apparently decided that I would be the centerpiece, literally, of this Romanian bath. I am standing in the cistern, surrounded by the others who are alternately pouring warm water over me and lightly lathering me with a fragrant oily soup. It is now dark and the candles offer only the slightest illumination. It is perfectly silent except for the bell-like melody of falling water.

With my eyes closed, I can distinguish one pair of hands from another, hands that without shyness traverse the surfaces of my body. The first hands I identify are Marina's, coarse and rough from her work with the stone of her sculpture, but aware of this, she touches softly. The hands moving most quickly, most impatiently have to be Paolina's. The competent steady plying hands are Angelika's, at work as if in the kitchen kneading dough. Giulia's touch is strange and tentative as if she's not really here. Sueno's is dreamy and as uncommitted as her pale gray eyes.

Within moments, I realize also that this is more than a bath, it is a ritual of initiation into whatever the 'order' is of this hilltop convent. At one point, while especially sensitive areas are anointed the sensation is so extreme I try to imagine what kind of sound could possibly express the giddy pleasure. At that instant, one of the island donkeys lets loose its crazy bray, like a Maine loon with hiccups and it sounds so like how I feel, I giggle, as do the others. After I am rinsed from the smaller amphorae around us, the others begin to douse and soap and rinse each other, and I join in making sure I have contact at least a little with everyone, in appreciation of my ritual bath.

Later, when we're eating a cold Greek supper on the terrace, I'm asked many questions by the others and it pleases me to feel their interest in me. I know so much of their stories, but to them I must be no more discernible than the Vulcan just visible out in the bay. I'm offered the one spare room in the convent to spend the night so I won't have to walk back in the dark to the villa.

I say, "I'd love to stay, but in the morning when I first wake, I always remember my dreams with my flute. I wake early, and I don't want to intrude on your peace here."

Everyone immediately insists I stay, insist they want to hear me play, insist they all rise early, so I agree.

Lying in bed I smile at the island silence, a joyous sense of well-being surrounding me, in the spirits of these remarkable women here at the convent. Their connection to Martin makes him alive in this room, in my mind, even in this bed. I feel an intense longing for him physically, as though we've been lovers for as long as I can remember. In spite of the fact that we've barely touched, he has entered me. This island and this villa are magic, a word I never use.

In the morning, I play my dream-induced music to the rising sun. I am standing at the window of my small cell-like room. The sun is just rising off to my right and illuminates the islands out front from the side, keeping one edge in shadow so they are sculpture-like. The same is true of the low clouds this morning, and because otherwise there is the same blue for both water and sky, with the horizon erased in the early morning haze, the clouds could be islands and the islands, clouds. So the music I play begins with this parity of islands and clouds and proceeds to the equality of these women of the convent and me. I feel so absorbed in their universe that I could be any one of them and they, me. That is my music this morning.

When I finish playing and walk from my room out to the terrace, they are all there. Some are sitting on low stone benches, some are standing facing different directions. But they all turn as one to look at me. Each wears a loose white tunic, and with the Aegean in the background, the thought comes to mind that this could be a Greek play, even though I've never seen one. Everyone observes me silently, and I wonder if they're waiting for me to speak my lines.

I smile and say, "Is there espresso?"

At this, everyone smiles and comes over. Surprisingly, Sueno is the first to speak, and since she speaks so rarely, everyone is quiet. She stands in front of me, her pale wise Romany eyes on mine, unblinking.

"Astra..."

She watches, her dusty-pink lips parted while she finds the words she wants... "Astra, that song you blew us..."

A small smile reveals bright white teeth. " It is like we are all one."

I say, "Islands and clouds, ocean and sky, Sueno."

Paolina has contained herself as long as she can and speaks rapidly...

"Astra, move in with us, that room you were in, we were all waiting for the perfect person, I'll make espresso for you every morning, and you have to admit we have wonderful baths."

Everyone laughs.

Then Giulia speaks with no smile.

"Here in the convent, you will be protected, no one falls here, out of towers or out of grace."

When I leave, I say that I'll think about their offer to adopt me into the convent, but I know in the end that I will decline, because my sweet, music-serving solitude has become too dear to me. At the age of thirty, I'm only willing to share my days and my nights with someone in exchange for love, passionate love on a level with art.

"Astra!"

I look to see Marina standing some distance behind me, calmly looking in my direction, though of course she can't see me. I'm some distance from the convent, sitting on a stone bench, and have been playing my flute. I wonder how she could have found her way here, the terrain is tricky, dangerous even.

"Oh, Marina, hello."

"I been listening to you play."

"Have you been there long? I didn't hear you coming."

"I'm here for a while, I start out from convent when I hear you play. This music, what do you think about this time when you play, Astra?"

"I was thinking about my mother."

"Ah, when I first hear you play, I too think about mother."

Marina stands silent while thoughts and images go through her mind. She is striking to look at. She's taken to wearing pale blue coveralls, that are covered with the white dust of the stone she carves. Her raven-black hair is long and in one thick ponytail tied behind her with a purple ribbon. Her large strong hands hang relaxed at her side. She is uniquely beautiful.

"Astra..."

"Yes, Marina?"

"I just few minutes ago have something magical happen to me as I make my way down here."

"Yes?"

"I almost afraid to say it, but I have flash of light behind my eyes while you play, can I come down where you are? Sit there?"

"Of course, but let me come get you. There is a deep crevice in front of you."

"Yes, I sense that."

I take Marina's hand with my bird hand, and she immediately says, "Oh your special hand, Astra."

"You Marina have two special hands."

And this is true. They are like the meaty underbelly of some soft animal that crawls across rocks all day. I lead her to the stone bench and we sit turned toward each other, our knees touching. Marina has skin as smooth as a child's, and her olive coloring is tinted rose on her cheeks from the Greek sun. Her dark eyes have a luminous brilliance, it's hard to believe she's blind.

"Okay I touch your face, Astra?"

"Of course, that's only fair since I've been looking at yours, you're very beautiful Marina." "You think so? Thank you. But you know, I have no mind picture of how I look. Even before I go blind here, I have not much picture of myself. You see, in monastery at Sucevița, we have no mirrors, too much for vanity, so for ten years, from when I twelve to when I twenty-two, I not once look at my face."

While Marina is talking, she is very lightly and carefully examining my features. The sensation is exquisite.

"You know Astra, when you come to bath night, I love touching you all over, because is only way for me to see you, have sense of you, but also because you are like sculpture I wish to make. You are so long and have both sharp angles and round places, really like my mother was, and you have nice big feet to keep sculpture steady.

"So that was you Marina, so thoroughly feeling my feet that night, I had my eyes closed the whole time."

"Yes, that me. Sometime to not see is not so terrible, yes?"

"Marina, you started to tell me about the light flash you just saw?"

"Well, I didn't really see it, yes, maybe you could say that. But what was so magical is that otherwise, ever since I go blind here, everything behind my eyes is black like night, all the time."

"How did it happen, your losing your sight?"

Marina's face clouds, and she turns away from me and is still for some time.

"I don't like to say this story, Astra, it very hard, because when I say it, I see it all in my head again, and otherwise behind my eyes is only black and that is peace."

"Of course, you don't have to tell me, Marina. I understand. My mother died when I was a child, too."

"How you know about my mother dying, Astra?"

"Martin told me."

I had decided to tell no one here at the villa how much Martin has told me about all of them, but the information about her mother seems right for Marina to know I know.

"He tell you my mother murdered?"

"Yes."

"Good, then I don't have to tell you that, I just say that one night, here at villa, sometime after Martin bring me here and we make his picture together, there is terrible storm with loud thunder and wild wind, the noise is horrible and is to me like what sound should have been when I see my mother killed, and that night, the picture in my mind of my mother killed is so clear, I can't look at it and I know I can never look at it again, and when I wake in the morning, I cannot see."

Marina has said all of this in seconds, as though to get it out and over with as quickly as possible. She sits now stoic and still. I pick up my flute and beginning with soft notes, I play to Marina. I play her a love song, no words I could ever come up with could express the complexity of feelings I have for her right now. She is so fragile and so fierce and so fine, so young to be imbued with such pain. She is so lovely, like a beautiful wild animal. As I play, I stand in front of her looking out over her head at the shimmering sea. She immediately wraps her strong arms around me and pulls me against her, her glossy black head turned and resting against my belly. My music increases in volume and there are high warbling notes that plead for, plead for, and then it strikes me as I hit the highest note of cry I can, my plan is so presumptuous, that in fear of jinxing it, I will not give it words. When I finish playing, Marina and I listen quietly to my last notes that are floating out over the bay, barely audible.

As Marina and I hold each other, I think of what Martin said about her, 'She freed me to love.' He would say no more. I wanted to ask him if they were lovers, but it seemed too invasive a question. I know now that they weren't, but Marina is like a fairy tale elf of love, exuding such sweet tenderness as to make one wish one could whisk her off for oneself, even while not knowing what in the world to do with her.

Two days later, Marina and I are walking down one of the cool corridors of the villa, toward Orlando's Brâncuşi room.

"You don't know about Brâncuşi, Marina? He too was Romanian, you know."

"No, I never hear of him, but I know nothing of other artists, except Martin of course."

I have told her about my mother being Brâncuşi's model and how he felt her body to help make his sculpting decisions.

"Ah..."

This is the first sound from Marina after several minutes of carefully exploring, with her hands, the three Brâncuşis. She has one hand on an angle and the other on a curve in the same sculpture.

"This like you, Astra, like sharp hip bone and round belly. You know, when I bathe you that night, I make sculpture in my mind."

She is quiet for a few more minutes and then says, "Maybe I could make sculpture of you Astra?... But maybe you won't like my sculptures when you see them, won't like what I might make you to be in my sculpture."

"Let me think about it, Marina. In the meantime, I'd love to see your sculptures, but you haven't invited me."

"You invited."

As we walk away from the villa, Marina says, "You know Astra, when you play to me that beautiful song the other day?..."

"Yes, Marina?"

"I have again flashes of light behind my eyes, a sweet light, I mean if I could smell that light it would be like lavender flower, you know? Isn't that magical?"

I am too excited to even think about this, so I just say, "That's nice Marina."

But I do feel my music has the power of Martin's paintings. Does that make Martin and me equals? Once again, I feel how strong the presence of Martin is on this island, and I still haven't seen the Annunciations, but I know the story of each. It is time to visit the chapel.

***

In the morning, I approach the Annunciation chapel with caution. I have brought my flute. I circle the round white building, blowing a few tentative notes. Art-to-art is my naive justification. When I open the door, the silence inside seems too studied, as though my approach has stilled whispering. The first image I see is Marina as Virgin, staring right at me. I gasp. Her presence is palpable.

I blow some loving notes to the virgin Marina, and seeing her looking at me, I feel certain I can do for her what I've presumptuously set out to do. Standing in the center of the room, I turn slowly. The room is flooded with soft morning light. The paintings are stunning. Everyone is here, Angelika, Hanna, Giulia, and of course dear Marina. But the strongest presence is Martin.

He may be somewhere on my island, but he is also here.

I even say, "Martin?" I'm surprised at the rush of warmth I feel as though he's here with me, alone in this chapel filled with his art.

While the sound of his name melds with the silent stone walls, I look at his paintings. Martin has made all the players his own, and even though they all retain the qualities I know of them in person, he has turned those qualities to his own use, to use in the power of his art.

In the first Annunciation, Angelika as the black-winged Archangel Gabriel is bringing her message to Hanna as Virgin. Angelika's hand is cupped over the exposed and protruding belly of the Virgin (Hanna was pregnant with Hans). In the second Annunciation, Angelika, again as Archangel, is bringing the word to Giulia as Virgin, who was pregnant with Nicolò. In this painting, I can see the strong, perceptive presence in Giulia that she had then and that drew Martin to her, before she slipped away into her present chrysalis of insanity. So sad. The third Annunciation consists of two dark, arched panels. In the first, Marina as black-winged Gabriel, is delivering her message to herself, as white-robed Virgin in the second panel. The Virgin Marina looks not at Gabriel (as the other Virgins do) but straight out at Martin as he painted her (and therefore at any viewer of this painting, thus making them a participant in the art). This created, as she said, Martin's own miracle. Art to alter people's lives, but I also sense that the paintings altered Martin's life. Especially the Marina diptych, because the two Marinas become one and it seems, one with Martin, and even I feel vaguely, one with me, and by extension I become one with Martin, and with this thought I'm surprised to feel strong physical arousal. Again, I say, "Martin?"

The effect of all this on me is unnerving, and I've seen as much as I can take at one time. As I'm leaving, I notice that opposite the three Annunciations, there is a narrow blank wall, forming a vertical rectangle, that seems to be there for something yet to come. I have a fleeting vision of myself, painted by Martin, immortalized by Martin, as surely this chapel and its images will outlast us all. I walk to the wall to place my hand on the cool stone, on myself, but I'm no longer there, my image is gone. For that I need Martin. Then I say it aloud, "I need Martin."

***

Marina's studio is an old stone storage building, whitewashed inside and out. She and I are standing by a low table that holds many small stone figures. While the form of these sculptures is interesting, they are very indecisive, very general and uncommitted.

I say gently, "Marina, these forms are beautiful, but it seems as though you haven't decided what you want them to be, or perhaps, who you want them to be."

"Astra, you say the truth, almost. I know who I want the sculpture to be, it is my mother, but I am afraid to make her. Whenever I feel her shape begin to come out of the sculpture, I stop."

I realize that Marina will have to have a new image of her mother to replace the murdered one in the memory of the twelve year-old daughter. She will have to have this new image in order to trust the restoration of her sight, which is now my obsession. And when I use this word, obsession, I immediately think of Martin because he used it so much to define the process of making his imagery. Again, I feel his presence.

Marina then turns to me and carefully moving her large inquiring hands down my face and onto my shoulders and then one in front and one in back down my body, she says, "Astra, like this Brâncuşi man do with your mother, maybe I do the opposite, I make you into my mother?"

She says this as a sad plea, with her face turned up to mine as though looking at me to see my answer, and at that instant I am certain I can achieve my goal, certain, because of the power of my music, and certain because of Marina's willingness to receive and embrace my music.

"Yes Marina, make me into your mother."

When I tell Orlando of my plan, he looks at me with raised eyebrows, but without disbelief.

He has come to believe in the alchemy of my music.

"Will you provide Marina with a beautiful block of marble, Orlando? When she finishes this work, and can see it, it must forever protect her from another vision of her murdered mother."

Orlando answers with his usual refined graciousness, "I would be honored to."

He arranges the delivery of a block of the world-famous marble from Paros, marble from the same quarry that supplied Michelangelo five centuries ago. This block, large enough for a full-size figure, comes by helicopter, a huge military helicopter. It is a surreal scene. Marina and I stand, holding hands, enveloped by the thump, thump of the huge gray-green machine descending from above to lower the marble carefully in the center of the paved courtyard by her studio.

"Astra, it like my mother coming down from heaven", Marina says, smiling through her tears.

***

I'm sitting on a stone bench, wearing a soft white cotton tunic. This is the position and the clothing that Marina wants, from her most vivid memory of her mother, when she was twelve and watched her mother sit like this as she told Marina the stories of various saints. We have been working for several weeks, and my form is beginning to emerge from the block of marble. Marina working steadily with mallet and chisel, comes over frequently to 'see me', as she says, with her inquisitive hands. She touches me both lightly for the forms of the fabric of my tunic, and more thoroughly for the form of my body. This tactile assessment of me is unabashed, and I know that Marina is thinking of her mother. But for me it is very sensual, Marina's hands are strong, her fingers agile, as she explores me for information, and, as she says, for inspiration. The aesthetic of my form is to be transcended into the soul of her mother, to imbue this block of gleaming marble with her spirit.

We work for hours at a time, and I would be bored if Marina was not so exquisite to look at. In her pale blue coveralls covered with white marble dust, her exotic dark beauty is startling. Her thick, ink-black hair tied behind, trails straight and shining to the small of her back. Her eyes, so dark, yet so filled with brilliance, trained on me or on the marble she caresses to gauge her progress, are so alive I think again it's hard to believe she cannot see.

When Marina's arms tire, I play to her while she rests sitting on the bench with me standing before her. This is the position we always take when I play, and, as usual, Marina leans her beautiful head against my belly. I play a riff of trills to try again to pierce the lifeless shadow behind her eyes, and to lend light to Marina until she has her own. As I play, my tremolos become tremors in Marina. And in response her fingers play a mute duet. She always cries when I do this and when I finish playing, I lean back to look at her. There are streaks through the pale marble dust on her cheeks, and splotches of wet dark blue in various patterns down the front of her coveralls, all of which intensify her beauty, and reinforce my will to do an act of God. As I say this to myself, I'm reminded that Martin's paintings performed the equivalent of an act of God and he was not shy about proclaiming that. This is how we've been spending our days, with Marina carving her block with increasing fervor. The form of her mother/Astra is gradually emerging and Marina is squinting more and more.

One morning, after we have worked for an hour, Marina suddenly backs away from the sculpture and childlike, puts her hands on her knees and leans forward, facing the marble. She looks very young, like a twelve-year-old, her lips parted in awe. Her expression is simultaneously one of joy and terror. This is the moment, I murmur to myself. I lift my flute to my lips and play to Marina so fervently it brings tears to my eyes. The notes are played to separate fear from joy, to discard the fear forever, and leave this tender Bucovinian girl charged with the conviction that she can see without reprisal.

"Oh," is all she says before turning to see me for the first time, then looking skyward to give God his due, before collapsing on the courtyard floor. When she comes to with the help of splashes of water, her eyes move left to right and then up to mine as I lean over her. Her sobs are mixed with giggles as she says, "So this is how you look like, Astra."

Later, I walk with Marina back to the convent, where she looks right at, and addresses each of the players by name. This causes pandemonium; Angelika believes it's a genuine miracle, and her Eastern Orthodox eyes lift skyward. Giulia too believes it's an act of God, but she is frightened by it and backs away from Marina. Paolina knows the power of art, and stares at me in awe. Only Sueno seems almost unaffected, and my guess is that to her it's all akin to some ancient Roma magic that she has experienced before, within her own milieu.

When Orlando hears about it, he says, "Astra, my dear, your art, your art, your art," and from a man whose whole life revolves around the power of art, I take this as a compliment. "Astra, I have the most wonderful news, Martin is on his way."

Orlando has interrupted my playing, and I'm momentarily disori-
ented. "Martin, on his way?"

"Yes, he's returning to Santorini, to the villa, with the children."

When the news sinks in, I'm confused. The only images I have of Martin are on my small island at home, and Martin on Santorini in the past as
he described it to me. I have never allowed myself the thought of him here
in the present, with me.

Orlando is puzzled by my response, or more accurately, my lack of
response. As is his style, he ponders me with eyebrows raised, his enormous eyes alert for clues.

I produce a smile and say, "That's wonderful news, it just took a minute to sink in, I was lost in my music."

He starts happily back down the hall. I call after him, "And Hanna?"

He turns and says, "Hanna it seems is returning to Germany, to her
world and her performance art. She felt she was losing her identity, and she
wanted to go alone. So Martin agreed to take responsibility for little Hans,
to keep her and Little Nicolò together, which is one reason I think he's coming back to the villa, filled as it is with surrogate mothers for the children.
I'm referring of course to the convent."

A week has passed.

From up here, the blue caique approaching the wharf, followed by its
narrow V seems like an arrow aimed at the heart of the villa. And it is. Martin and the children are aboard, and the whole cast of the villa is waiting on
the wharf below. I am alone up here on the elevator platform. My music is
a soft inquiry into my own heart, which is flooded to overflowing, not only
because of Martin with the children bringing themselves, but bringing with
them an aura of my own little island. I look down two hundred feet to the

wharf and watch the choreography of the greetings. Little Nicolò is dashing from person to person, each trying to hold him, but he seems determined to greet everyone simultaneously. Little by little, Hans is dipping and swinging and staring into each set of eyes. Martin is first enveloped by Orlando, and then by the others. Finally, he leans toward Orlando to say something. Orlando looks up at me and points. Martin, with one hand shielding his eyes from the sun, waves to me, and I to him.

Everyone is on the antiques terrace tonight, even Giulia, who consistently calls Martin, Nicolò. I am sitting on a stone bench with little Nicolò on one side and little Hans on the other, each holding my bird hand which is relaxed in my lap, although it occasionally moves on its own with the impulse to play a joyous sonata to accompany this gathering.

Gin flows, then the Santorini wine that accompanies course after course of culinary artistry. Martin didn't want to move inside to the dining room, didn't want to leave what he calls this Greek theater. And theater it is. Even the ancient marble sculptures seem like bit players, lit as we all are by some Goddess of Illumination out there hiding behind the low clouds, sending out chromatic spotlights onto each of us as we make our moves and say our lines. As I watch Martin, whose attention is constantly sought by one player after another, he now seems like the most familiar person in my life. I know so much about him, because of everyone here connected to him. Did he intend that, by telling me so much and then sending me here? He and I look at each other off and on midst the happy chaos of the evening. And when we do, my bird hand flutters and the children look down as though expecting it to take flight and circle the terrace. Finally, very late, long after the children are in bed, and most of the convent dwellers have left, we stragglers head off to bed.

By my room in the dark hallway, Martin puts his arms around me. I hold onto him and we make some little adjustments so that we're as neatly fitted together as possible. Our hearts send beats back and forth. Finally, he steps back, places his painting hand on my cheek and says, "Astra, I'm so glad I'm here, I feel..."

But he doesn't have the words. Nor do I, so I just put my bird hand on his cheek. He shivers slightly.

"Good night, Martin." "Good night, Astra."

We kiss, each intending it to be a European kiss of right cheek and then left cheek, but between the two, our tongues, previously tongue-tied now tie around each other, curled and as alive as slippery sea creatures from long before the age of man urged on by Darwinian insistence. There is a pause and then an unstated agreement that whatever is to come next, this is not the place for it, and we know where that will be.

In the morning, I wake early and decide not to play on my terrace for fear of waking those who have just gone to bed a few hours ago. I wander out beyond the villa, through the olive grove and to the Annunciation chapel. When I open the door, there, once more is the image of Marina staring at me just as she stared at Martin as he painted her, and just as she has been staring at me since she recovered her sight. The rest of the players in the Annunciations are occupied with observing each other. I back away from them as far as I can to see all three paintings together. This puts my back against the last blank wall in the museum, where I envisioned myself painted by Martin. I'm wearing a light translucent cotton shift that hangs loose. I lean back against the wall and the cool smooth surface is soothing.

I begin to play very soft notes, so soft it's more like melodic breathing. I've never played so softly before, and I realize as I close my eyes that this is the sound of my life since the morning I first saw little Nicolò and Hans up at the tree line when I was playing below at the water's edge. This is the sound of all these players, the sound of their spectral presence in my mind and in my music. As I play, I again imagine myself painted on this wall by Martin.

"Astra."

Martin is now standing close. I keep my eyes closed. I sense more than feel his breath coming to me to be met by mine. While our breaths explore each other, we wait as though for permission to proceed, permission from the images surrounding us. I arch my back and Martin's hands encircle me. My flute is moved from my mouth by Martin or by me, I don't know who, and is replaced by his lips. I am pressed against the wall by Martin's body, firmly, as though to form an imprint forever. I have trouble breathing, and realizing this, Martin says, "Astra, I'm sorry, I just had this compelling image of you, or rather image of your image, and the two became one in my mind."

He is standing back, assessing the moment, and I realize again how obsessive this man is. I also realize again that his life and his art are one and the same, which is reassuring. I lean abruptly against the wall, pulling Martin to me, and leaving the floor like the seraph I'm soon to be, wrap my legs around him, and quickly sheathe him so tightly, our lives seem as interlocked as our flesh. Our fervent sounds form no words and I don't know how much time passes before we slump to the floor almost unable to catch our breath.

When finally we are still, Martin says, "Astra, I want to paint you on this wall, just as you were, flute to your lips, to make you the witnessing seraph to these Annunciations, and more importantly, witness to me."

This final intimacy pleases me; Martin has entered my mind to know my wish.

***

Two days later I am standing with my back to the plastered wall that will host the fresco of Astra as angel of music. My flute is to my lips. I'm blowing a soft prelude to the painting to come. Martin's plan is to paint me life-size. At this moment he is tracing my outline with charcoal onto the white plaster. His hand silhouetting me is gentle and moves in and out of my curves and I have a brief image of Brâncuşi doing the same with my mother. I remind Martin of Brâncuşi and my mother, and he laughs softly and adds, "My sense of transcendence is not so saintly."

Each morning as Martin and I work on the fresco, the domed museum is filled with indirect light, and it's like being suspended in a cylinder of luminous liquid. For Martin, who is in his obsessed painter mode, it is a process of completing what Orlando joyously refers to as Martin's magnum opus. His power of concentration is so strong, it's as though he's alone in this space. He even occasionally mutters to himself.

For me, the opposite is true. I am at peace and open to all around me, watching him carefully as his genius pours out, and I'm looking carefully at Angelika as Archangel Gabriel and Hanna and Giulia as the Virgin Mary, and especially at Marina as Virgin, who looks out directly at me.

Martin has asked me to play while he paints me with my flute to my lips. I play to him and to each of the others living forever now on the walls of this chapel. But especially I play to Marina, the music I played to her as she recovered her vision while carving the sculpture of her mother.

What an interesting loop, I think, between all of us and the grace of art, out of which has come the birth of Hans, the birth of Nicolò, the restored sight of Marina, and Martin's final understanding of the meaning to him of the Annunciation, where Angel Marina announces to Virgin Marina the miracle of creation, which to Martin means the miracle of art. And now, he and I are together, and he's blessing me with inclusion here, in his own small Greek temple.

When we finish our work on the fresco each day, we make love right on the floor, here in front of all these painted witnesses, including my own emerging image, and it is exotically erotic, especially myself on the wall observing myself on the floor in the fervent passion that Martin and I ignite on the cool smooth marble. It's as though we're trying to press our own images into the last remaining blank surface.

At the end of three weeks, I stand before the completed painting. In this fresco, I am wearing a white gown, fitted high at my waist and my skin is pale. My lightness seems to be an aura of the white stone wall. Only my black hair, parted from my high round forehead, and my blue-black eyes offer contrast. I have gold wings, real gold, gold leaf from fragile sheets Martin has burnished into the gesso on the wall. Because my feet are a few inches above the floor, these gold wings hold me in a moment of ascension. My silver flute is held to my lips and I can hear in my mind the music I played to Martin as he painted me. He has painted my bird hand as a pale blur of tremolo. The direction of my gaze is indeterminate, I could be looking at any of the three Annunciation paintings. I am painted in a simplified, slightly Byzantine style that creates a sense of timelessness appropriate to the site of this small museum on this ancient island.

***

Six months have passed. Martin and I, with Nicolò and Hans, live like a family. It has evolved seamlessly and wordlessly, as a truth in no need of words, words that surely would have been inadequate.

Hans is now my music student. It came about quite by accident. One morning, I heard a faint odd mixture of sounds coming from the olive grove behind the villa. As I got closer, I saw Hans sitting with crossed legs under the canopy of an old gnarled tree. She was holding one of my flutes against her mouth in a perfect imitation of my posture, playing. I have three flutes

and this was my Japanese wood flute. She was blowing adamantly and pro
ducing eerie whistling sounds. She was also crying from the frustration of
not being able to produce an actual note, because her lips were in the wrong
position. Tears were streaming down her cheeks, as she sent her whistling
like a gale created by a Greek god of musical storms.

I approached her slowly and when she saw me she stopped blowing
and stared at me, her expression a mix of thwarted will and guilt at being
found with my flute. I knelt before her, took the flute from her quivering
hand, and moved it to my mouth. With my eyebrows raised to say, watch,
this is the way it's done, I blew a soft pure note. Then I handed the flute
back to her, and amazingly, she not only blew a perfect note, but the exact
one I had blown. Her eyes opened wide and her eyebrows shot up in cele-
bration.

That was how it started, and we didn't move from the olive grove for
the whole day. Little Nicolò brought food and tea out to us twice. By evening, Hans was combining clear notes in small improvisations of her own.
More importantly, it became clear to all of us, including Hans, that she was
now, for the first time in her life learning a language to communicate with
the rest of the world.

That night we all went to sleep to the sound of Hans's flute, and woke
to new Hans compositions in the morning. She was exhausted but trembling with excitement at her discovery. I gave Hans the flute, told her it was
hers to keep, and she linked her arm in mine and led me to where I keep
my flutes and gestured that we play together, and we did. I played to her
and she played to me, and it was the first conversation Hans had in her
lifetime with another human being, but not the last. We didn't know then
the effect Hans's music would have on everyone she encountered in the
future.

The most intense improvisation I hear her play is to Hanna, who one day just appeared at the villa with a German performance troupe she was traveling with. Hanna is affectionate with Hans, but also seems remote. Hans's music is a kind of plea, as though she is asking Hanna where do I stand with you, mother? The passages end in high notes, like question marks. They are also rich and moving. Hanna is soon strongly affected and she and her group create performance pieces in response to Hans's playing. Hans is enthralled, and strangely, becomes a kind of director, because the others only move and mime in response to her playing. The pieces are quirky and appealing and are different each time. They also hint at a power that will be revealed only later. Hanna begins to show intense affection and pride toward Hans which has Hans practically swooning with love for her mother.

A few days later, Hanna tells us she and her troupe are leaving for California, and taking Hans with them as part of their traveling theater. Hans is thrilled with her new mission in life, and even more thrilled to be with her mother again, although she constantly watches her warily as though she might disappear again at any moment.

Nicolò is of course devastated by the impending loss of Hans, but when asked if he wants to go with Hanna also, he declines. He has become too attached to Martin. He says, "I'm going to stay with my dad." He is, I think, afraid of how easily Hanna has come and gone in the past. Not to mention the disappearance of his own mother into her ethereal world. She's there and she's not there. A lot for an emerging adolescent to deal with. I'm pleased he's staying, I'm beginning to think of him as my son, and more importantly, as our son, Martin and me.

Nicolò does, however, at dinner the last night everyone is together, turn to Hans and say, with studied maturity, "You know, I'll come find you someday."

The morning Hanna and her group leave with Hans, Martin, and Nicolò and I stand together on the wharf until the departing caique has rounded the peninsula, and the rumble of the engine has wafted away in the clear morning air. I think about all that has been brought about by the paintings of Martin, and the sculpture of Marina, and now the music of Hans. I raise my flute to my lips to play a paean to the power of art, and at the end I blow so softly it could be just the sound of my Brâncuşi bird hand, ascending, ascending, ascending.

Part Three

Epilogue

Every few days, I am propelled in my wheel chair, out to the Annunciation chapel to again view the great paintings of my late, dear friend, Martin. These paintings over time have been recognized by museum curators and directors all over Europe as monumental in importance because of the power of the metaphor and the quality of the painting. The American museums, unable to transcend the word 'anachronism,' have once again flaunted their provincialism. The American director of the Guggenheim in Balboa condescended to request a visit, after hearing so much from other curators about the 'Santorini Annunciations.' When the first syllable of the 'A' (for anachronism) word escaped his lips, I said, "Sir, if your own collection were not housed in a structure resembling the aftermath of a giant can opener gone berserk, you would be able to see what you cannot see."

Yes, the death of *The Annunciationist*, as Angelika, my longtime cook and model for his Gabriel, called Martin, was indeed a severe blow to all of us. The French Foreign Legion would have said he died in the line of duty. But more about that later.

So the lives that are works of art around me, indulge me by taking turns delivering me to the blue-domed home of Martin's paintings, and again telling me their individual tales (I almost said fairy tales and I could have) of the effect of Martin's art upon them. But more about that later. I know, 'More about that later', 'More about that later'. But you see, I have to live long enough to tell the whole story, or no one will know, so please forgive and indulge me, by letting me take my time. Trust me, I'm in no hurry to abandon my brief existence in the many millennia of Greek drama preceding me.

First, let me deal with the saddest of the news, the demise of Martin.

Martin and Astra, he with his painter's hand, she with her musical bird hand, settled into the villa to produce their remarkable art. The intensity of their love for each other matched the intensity of their art. Martin had told me years ago that it was the process of painting the Annunciations, and what he realized about himself as he completed them, that freed him to love Astra with such total abandon. He was right. I remembered how lost he was when he first arrived here, how driven by a vague quest.

One year ago, he was contacted by a descendent of the Medici (yes, those Medici), and asked to paint a fresco in the tower of a Medici castle outside of Florence where this Medici and his young wife resided. The tower extended up from their bedroom. The Medici wanted his wife pregnant, but had not been able to achieve his goal, in spite of much medical consultation. Martin was asked to paint an Annunciation angel on the wall, descending from the top of the tower. This Medici was obsessive, and later it was also realized, somewhat deranged. He had heard the reports of the result of Martin's Annunciations on Santorini, that is, the pregnancies of Giulia and Hanna. He believed that Martin had the powers of the original Archangel Gabriel. And because this man was a descendent of the Medici who became Pope (Pope Leo X), he thought he had special connections.

Martin was skeptical at first about the whole project, but the Medici pursued him relentlessly, obsessively, and eventually Martin remarked to all of us only half-jokingly, "How could I turn down the patronage of the Medici, even Michelangelo couldn't do that."

Astra was in the midst of recording for a new CD, so Martin went alone to Florence to meet the fate of so many before him in their dealings with the Medici.

The tower extended thirty feet above the bedroom, and a scaffolding was built to Martin's specifications. As inspiration for Martin, The Medici specified that his wife, attired in white, lie in the bed beneath him, in the role of the Virgin. Martin was amused by this and only said, 'Fine, but watch out for dripping paint.'

As it turned out, dripping paint was the least the wife had to watch out for. In the course of the weeks Martin spent painting the fresco and interacting with his patrons, the wife fell in love with Martin. She told her husband of lying beneath the artist in a state of sexual arousal that she was sure would result in her husband's wish that she become pregnant.

In true Medici tradition, the husband had a servant finesse the scaffolding so that it suddenly collapsed, with Martin plunging thirty feet to be killed along with (or more accurately, on top of) Signora Medici.

I can make light of this, only now, after a year of grieving, because Martin would have had it that way. In his painting and his life, he lived five centuries in the past, and nobody got off scot-free then. I can hear him chuckle as I say this. And also, knowing of my own imminent demise, he would empathize.

Astra, on the other hand, has not yet recovered. All her music since has been in the realm of death dirge. It is beautiful, but terribly sad. That was the past, and we've all absorbed it.

The present is, what shall I say, going to be brief, because I have suddenly taken a turn for the worse. My unique combination of internal organ complications, seemingly all unrelated, have now reached a consensus:

they will all cooperate to send me on my way before the fearsome pain pre-
dicted by my old Greek friends, the doctors attending me, makes its appearance.

The future, I'm pleased to say, is the last transcendent work of art of
my life (well, to be technically correct, my death). The image is clear, very
clear, because I have nothing else to experience, because, well, I'm dead.
I'm granting you the point of view I'm blessed with, that is the view from
above, above, but close enough for us to see all the details:

The three fishermen, whose caiques have so loyally serviced the needs
of the villa, have all kindly scrubbed their boats clean for the watery procession across to Nea Kameni. In the first caique, I lie wrapped in an ancient
woven white shroud, on a simple wood platform with four long wood han-
dles, two in front, and two in back. Standing at the stern of the boat, are
Astra and Hans, each holding her flute. In the two caiques following are
Angelika, Marina, Giulia, Nicolò, Paolina, Sueno, Hamm, Reginald, and
Henrietta.

Everyone has agreed to wear black, which is just brilliant. As the boats
pull away from the dock of the villa, motoring slowly across to the Vulcan,
the bright blue dome of the Annunciation Chapel is overlooking everything. Astra and Hans begin to play their improvised requiem, music of
indescribable depth, filled as it is with the history of all of us.

The residents of Santorini have lined the various roads and terraces
overlooking the bay. The island police have kindly agreed not to observe,
because of course what we are doing is against the law.

Upon reaching the shore, I am carefully lifted from the caique by everyone. There is just room for each to have a hand on the poles of my platform. Zigzagging slowly up to the crest of the Vulcan, there is huffing and
puffing. I've not gotten any smaller in my last days. At the top, I'm set down

on the cusp of the deep volcanic cavity. Wisps of steam and smoke lift eerily past everyone. Astra and Hans play their last paean to Orlando Pettingill. As the final notes soar skyward, my platform is tilted abruptly, and it and I dive down to finally find, or not, my own final Atlantis. Only I will know.

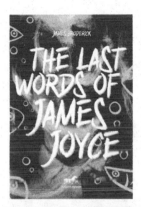

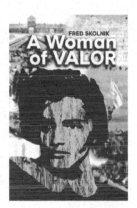
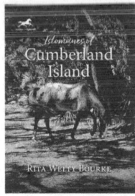
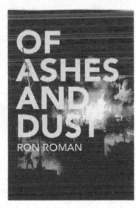